Knights of Tabor

A Manual of the Knights of Tabor

and Daughters of the tabernacle

Knights of Tabor

A Manual of the Knights of Tabor
and Daughters of the tabernacle

ISBN/EAN: 9783337286774

Printed in Europe, USA, Canada, Australia, Japan

Cover: Foto ©Andreas Hilbeck / pixelio.de

More available books at **www.hansebooks.com**

A MANUAL

OF THE

KNIGHTS OF TABOR,

AND

DAUGHTERS OF THE TABERNACLE,

INCLUDING THE

CEREMONIES OF THE ORDER, CONSTITUTIONS, INSTALLATIONS, DEDICATIONS, AND FUNERALS, WITH FORMS,

AND THE

TABORIAN DRILL AND TACTICS.

BY

MOSES DICKSON, P.G.M.,

Founder of the Order of Twelve.

ST. LOUIS, MO.
1879.

Entered according to Act of Congress, in the year 1879, by
MOSES DICKSON,
In the office of the Librarian of Congress, at Washington.

INTRODUCTION.

Orders, societies, and governments were instituted for the purpose of making a united effort in a given direction. What one man cannot accomplish, many men united can. Hence great enterprises for the well-being of mankind are carried forward by companies. Governments are formed by uniting a number of people under one form or code of laws. Societies are organizations of a number of persons to accomplish a certain object or to obtain a desired end. Man was made a social being; he must have society, or the company of a fellow-being, or he will drift into barbarism and brutality. Man is an intelligent being. Civilization, art, science, and architecture and government, must come only from a united effort. Therefore, the Order of Twelve, that the members may form one band of brothers, united by the strongest of ties, — friendly interest, love, and brotherhood, — do agree to form an organization to be called the Knights of Tabor, or the Order of Twelve, and hereby pledge our word on oath to each other, in the name of our Omnipotent Father, to be governed by the following Constitution:

HISTORY.

The Order of Knights of Tabor was founded in the city of Galena, Ill., A. D. 1855, and known by the name of the Order of Twelve. The names of the organizers were A. H. Richardson, William P. Emery, James T. Smith, J. G. Johnson, R. H. Cain, and Moses Dickson. During the years of 1856–57–58–59 the Order was established in many of the Southern States, and known by various names, yet the signs and passwords were the same. Many of the old members now living, who have passed through years of suffering and trials, will remember the words of comfort and advice we received in our Temples or Lodges. In the darkest hours just before the breaking out of the civil war, our links were fixed at all the news centres, so that in a few hours, in every hamlet, and in every town, city, and plantation, the members of our Order kept the people posted on that which interested us most. How was it that the colored people all through the Southern States knew every movement at the North? The old members of the Order can tell you of a system of telegraphing unknown to Prof. Morse, by which we reached every man and woman, and prepared them for coming events. In the conflict and during the war, and the changing of residences of many of the leading members, the Order gradually went to sleep. It is said that good institutions never die. Just so. The Temple of the Knights of Tabor has again opened her door, to stand open as long as the Order can benefit man. We call on the old members that have been spared to life from the battle-fields of the great rebellion. You are called to rally once more under the banner of the Knights of Tabor. Many of our number fell battling for freedom, and their bodies lie beneath the sod of many battle-fields. May the Great Giver of eternal life give them eternal happiness. Brothers, let the germ of the Order be watered with life; let us perpetuate the Temple; let us take up the old cry, "Linked to each other in friendship's bonds, hand in hand through life we will go." Our WORD, "Break every chain of injustice." Our trust is in God, the Ruler in the counsels and governments of men.

Brother! Friend! We greet you! Push the Order onward.

MOSES DICKSON,
P. G. Mentor.

CONSTITUTION

OF THE

NATIONAL GRAND TEMPLE AND TABERNACLE

OF THE

KNIGHTS OF TABOR.

FOUNDED, A. D. 1855.

FORM OF GRAND TEMPLE.

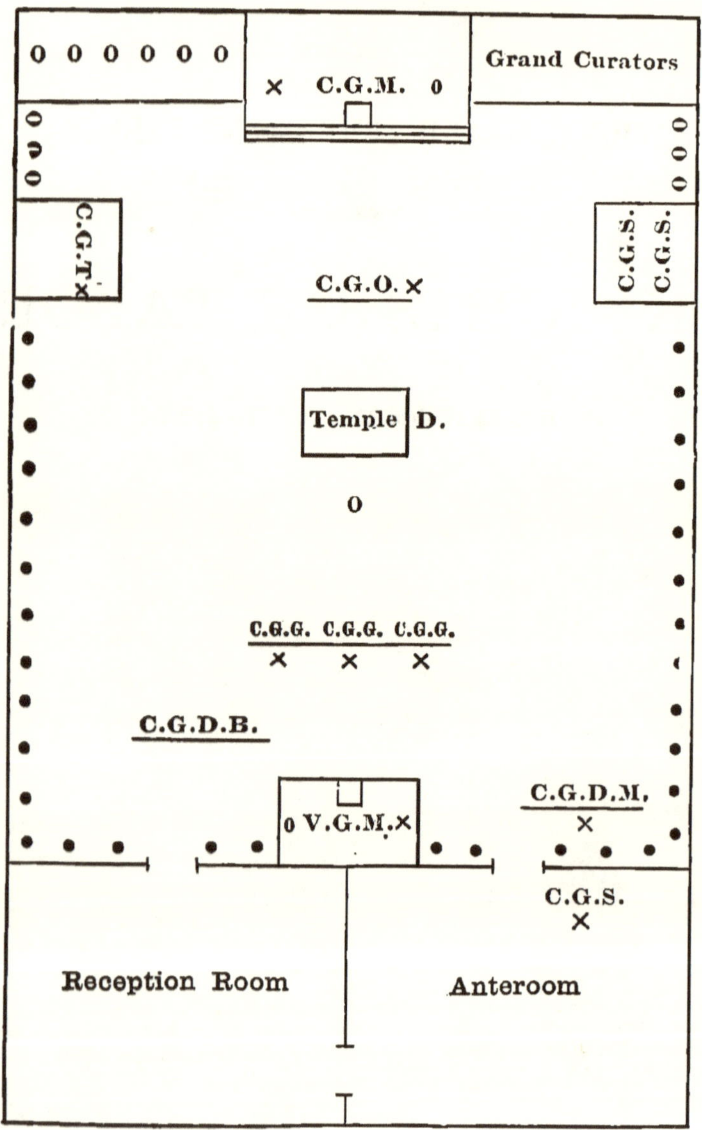

CONSTITUTION.

ARTICLE I.

This organization shall be known as the Knights of Tabor, or the Order of Twelve, of the United States of North America.

ARTICLE II.

FORM OF GOVERNMENT.

Section 1. There shall be a National Grand Temple, and any number of subordinate Temples and Tabernacles.

Sec. 2. The places of meeting for the Knights shall be called Temples; and the meetings of the Daughters shall be called Tabernacles.

ARTICLE III.

THE NATIONAL GRAND TEMPLE.

Section 1. The National Grand Temple shall be composed of all Past Grand Mentors, and the Chief Mentors and Vice-Mentors and Past Mentors of all subordinate Temples; and Chief and Past Preceptresses of Tabernacles.

Sec. 2. The Chief Tribune of a Tabernacle shall

be a member of the Grand Temple during his term of office.

Sec. 3. A Temple shall have three votes in the Grand Temple; a Tabernacle shall have three votes; each member shall have one vote, and each officer shall have one vote. The Chief Grand Mentor shall have the casting vote in case of a tie.

ARTICLE IV.

JURISDICTION.

Section 1. The National Grand Temple shall have jurisdiction over all Temples of the Knights of Tabor and Tabernacles of Daughters in the United States; and enacting laws, granting charters and warrants, and suspending charters or warrants for proper causes; to receive and hear appeals, and to redress grievances and complaints arising in the Temples or Tabernacles, and to provide for its support and government.

Sec. 2. The National Grand Temple shall hold annual sessions on the second Tuesday in August, at ten o'clock, A. M., and thereafter as the Grand Temple may determine.

Sec. 3. Special sessions may be called by the Chief Grand Mentor whenever he may deem it necessary; or it shall be his duty to call a special session when requested by one-third of the subordinate Temples and Tabernacles.

ARTICLE V.

OFFICERS.

1. A Chief Grand Mentor—C. G. M.
2. A Vice-Grand Mentor — V. G. M.
3. A Chief Grand Scribe — C. G. S.
4. An Assistant Grand Scribe — A. G. S.
5. A Chief Grand Treasurer — C. G. T.
6. A Chief Grand Orator — C. G. O.
7. A Chief Grand Drill-Master — C. G. D. M.
8. A Chief Grand Color-Bearer — C. G. C. B.
9. A Chief Grand Guard — C. G. G.
10. A Chief Grand Guard — C. G. G.
11. A Chief Grand Guard — C. G. G.
12. A Chief Grand Sentinel — C. G. St.

ARTICLE VI.

DUTIES OF OFFICERS.

SECTION 1. The Chief Grand Mentor shall preside at all meetings of the National Grand Temple; he shall have power to call special sessions when he determines that it is needed; he shall enforce order, decide all questions of order, appoint officers *pro tem.*, in case of the absence or disqualification of the officer elect; he can give permission, by dispensation, in all cases requiring a temporary suspension of the rules, laws, and regulations of the National Grand Temple; he can organize Temples of the

Knights of Tabor, or Tabernacles or Daughters, either in person or by deputy; he can confer the degrees of the Temple and Tabernacle, or deputize the power by commission; he can constitute new Temples and Tabernacles by charter or warrant, install their officers, dedicate Temples and Tabernacles, visit and preside in any Temple or Tabernacle. He shall visit annually all Temples and Tabernacles, either in person or by deputy; he shall appoint all committees that are not otherwise ordered; he can order the Chief Grand Scribe and the Chief Grand Treasurer, with their books, in his presence, to inspect the condition of the National Grand Temple; he shall report annually to the Grand Session the condition of all Temples and Tabernacles, and the number of new Temples and Tabernacles; he shall sign all drafts on the Grand Treasurer, and all other papers that may require his signature to make them authentic.

SEC. 2. He shall furnish new Temples with charters and books, and new Tabernacles with warrants and books; he shall report to the Chief Grand Scribe, monthly, the names and number of the Temples and Tabernacles that have been chartered and warranted, with name and address of the Chief Mentor, and the Chief Preceptress, and with the monthly report he shall pay to the C. G. S. all money that he has received for charters, warrants, and books;

he shall, at the annual session, give account of all the property of the National Grand Temple that is in his possession, and recommend such additions as are needed; he shall turn over to his successor all the property that he has belonging to the National Grand Temple; he shall, in his annual address, make such recommendations as he thinks will benefit the order.

VICE GRAND MENTOR.

SEC. 3. In the absence of the C. G. M., the V. G. M. shall preside over the National Grand Temple; and in case of the absence of both, the National Grand Temple shall proceed to elect a C. G. M. *pro tem.* In the absence of the C. G. M. out of the United States, or by death, or by physical or mental inability to fulfil his duty, the V. G. M. shall perform and fulfil all the duties of the C. G. M. until the regular annual session.

CHIEF GRAND SCRIBE.

SEC. 4. The C. G. S. shall have charge of the records, journal, register, and papers, and preserve the archives; he shall have the power to provide his office with all the necessary books and stationery to enable him to perform his duties; he shall keep a journal of the business of the Grand Temple and the proceedings of the Grand Session; he shall keep a register of all Temples and Tabernacles, with date of their charter and warrant, with the name of the town or city, county, and state where they are situated; he shall keep a record of all members of the Grand Temple; he shall keep in his office a copy of the seal of each subordinate Temple and Tabernacle, attest all official papers and documents with the seal of his office; he shall receive and give notice to all the subordinate Temples and Tabernacles of all rejected candidates, and of members that have been suspended or expelled; he shall attend to and carry on the correspondence of the Grand Temple, and give notice to the Temples and Tabernacles when and where to meet the Grand Temple; he shall perform such other duties as are assigned to him by the Grand Temple; he shall receive all moneys coming to the Grand Temple, and pay them over to the G. T. without delay, taking his receipt; draw all drafts on the Grand Treasurer, and attest them; keep his accounts ready for examination at any time; he shall, at the expiration of his term of office, deliver to his successor all books, papers, and other property belonging to the Grand Temple. His salary shall be regulated from time to time by the Grand Temple.

ASSISTANT GRAND SCRIBE.

SEC. 5. It shall be the duty of the A. G. S. to attend to the business of the C. G. S. in his absence, and in case of the death, removal, resignation, inability, or absence out of the United States of the C. G. S., the official duties shall devolve on the A. G. S. until the annual session.

CHIEF GRAND TREASURER.

Sec. 6. It shall be the duty of the C. G. T. to receive all moneys and valuables belonging to the Grand Temple, and keep a correct account of the same; he shall pay drafts only when signed by the C. G. M. and countersigned by the C. G. S.; he shall make an annual report to the Grand Temple of the business of his office; his book shall be open for the inspection of the C. G. M., or any committee that he may appoint, at all times; he shall give to the C. G. S. a receipt for all moneys he receives; his books shall show the amount of moneys received and paid out; he shall give a statement, in writing, at the Grand Session, exhibiting the amounts of his receipts and the amounts of his disbursements, and for what purpose the money was drawn; at the expiration of his term of office, he shall deliver all books, papers, and cash that belong to the Grand Temple to his successor.

CHIEF GRAND ORATOR.

Sec. 7. The C. G. O. shall officiate at the altar and lead the devotional exercises of the Grand Temple, and perform the part of Chaplain on all public and private occasions. He shall be furnished with a commission by the C. G. M., constituting him a District Deputy.

CHIEF GRAND DRILL-MASTER.

Sec. 8. It shall be the duty of the C. G. D. M. to perform the duties of a marshal on all occasions; to form and conduct all public processions of the Grand Temple. He shall have charge of the inside door of the Grand Temple, and perform its duties.

CHIEF GRAND COLOR-BEARER.

Sec. 9. It shall be the duty of the C. G. C. B. to have care and possession of the Grand Colors of the Grand Temple, and to carry the Grand Colors in all processions and ceremonies of the Order.

CHIEF GRAND GUARD.

Sec. 10. It shall be the duty of the C. G. G. to attend to the inside of the Grand Temple, and, under the instruction of the C. G. M., keep order, and convey messages from the inner to the outer Temple.

CHIEF GRAND SENTINEL.

Sec. 11. It shall be the duty of the C. G. St. to guard the outer door of the Temple when in session, and see that none enter but members of the Order.

ARTICLE VII.

BOARD OF GRAND CURATORS.

Section 1. The Board of Grand Curators shall consist of seven members of the Grand Temple, elected annually at the Grand Session. They shall be corporators of the Grand Temple. The incorporation shall be held in their name. All donations, devises, or gifts for the Grand Temple, or for the benefit of any subordinate Temple or Tabernacle, shall be made to them. They shall invest in such stock, loans, or securities the funds of the Grand Temple as the Grand Temple may direct. They shall call in, sell, and realize on such loans, stocks, and investments, under the orders of the Grand Temple; collect interest, dividends, rents, and all money arising or accruing from any investments belonging to the Grand Temple; pay all money that they collect to the C. G. S., or, if for the benefit of a subordinate Temple or Tabernacle, they shall pay to the C. S. or C. R. The C. G. M. shall be a member and chairman of the Board. The Grand Temple shall furnish the Board with such books and stationery as they may need. They shall make an annual report to the Grand Temple of all their business, and, at the expiration of their term of office, they shall deliver to their successors all books, securities, deposits, stocks, papers, deeds, and money that belong to the Grand Temple or subordinate Temple or Tabernacle. They shall audit the accounts of the C. G. S. and the C. G. T., at the annual session, and report during the session.

ARTICLE VIII.

BONDS.

Section 1. The C. G. S. and the C. G. T. shall, before entering upon the duties of their offices, give a bond, with such security as shall be determined by the Grand Temple, to the Board of Curators, for the faithful application of all moneys belonging to the Grand Temple, in accordance with the laws or orders of the Grand Temple.

ARTICLE IX.

DISTRICT GRAND MENTORS.

Section 1. The D. G. M.'s are appointed by the C. G. M. Their duties and districts are defined in their commissions.

ARTICLE X.

ELECTION OF GRAND OFFICERS.

Section 1. The officers of the Grand Temple shall be elected during the annual session, and installed before the session closes.

Sec. 2. The ballots shall be written. A majority of all votes cast shall be necessary to elect. The nomination shall be made in open session. In case no candidate receives a majority on the first ballot, the candidate receiving the lowest number of votes shall be dropped, and so on in each succeeding ballot until one is elected.

SEC. 3. The C. G. M. shall appoint three tellers, whose duty it is to count the ballots and announce the result.

ARTICLE XI.

PERPETUATION.

SECTION 1. In case of the death, resignation, inability or disqualification, or the absence out of the United States of the C. G. M. and V. G. M., the C. G. S. shall call a meeting of the Board of Curators, who shall elect a C. G. M. to serve the balance of the term, of which notice shall be given by them to all Temples and Tabernacles.

ARTICLE XII.

POWER AND AUTHORITY.

SECTION 1. The National Grand Temple shall be the only legitimate source of authority to enact laws, regulations, and rules for the government of the National Grand Temple, and the Temples and Tabernacles chartered and warranted by its authority. It has the positive power to investigate and determine all business or matter relating to Temples of the Knights of Tabor and Tabernacles of Daughters, or individual members; to exercise a general supervision over the business and work of Temples and Tabernacles.

Sec. 2. Any member of Temple or Tabernacle who has been suspended or expelled shall have the right to appeal to the Grand Temple. Such an appeal is made in writing, and filed with the C. G. S. The appellant is hereby required to give notice to the appellee, or no action can be taken or had thereon.

ARTICLE XIII.

DELINQUENT, SUSPENDED, AND DISSOLVED.

Section 1. Any Temple or Tabernacle may be suspended or dissolved, and its charter or warrant forfeited to the Grand Temple, (1) for neglecting or refusing to obey the constitution, rules, and regulations of the Grand Temple; (2) for refusing or neglecting to make the returns to the annual Grand Session for two years, or the non-payment of dues; (3) for neglecting to hold regular stated or monthly meetings, unless prevented by some unforeseen circumstance; (4) by its membership diminishing to less than a working or constitutional quorum.

Sec. 2. When a Temple or Tabernacle is suspended or dissolved, it shall be the duty of its senior officer to deliver to the C. G. M. or the Grand Temple the charter or warrant, books, emblems, furniture, regalias, and other property.

SEC. 3. Members of any defunct Temple or Tabernacle, who were in good standing at the time of dissolution, can be received into any Temple or Tabernacle by presenting the C. G. M. certificate, and paying the admission fee. The application for such certificate must be accompanied with fee of $1.

SEC. 4. All effects and funds received by the Grand Temple from suspended or dissolved Temples or Tabernacles shall be restored when the Grand Temple, by a majority vote, at a stated or special session, reinstates such Temple or Tabernacle.

ARTICLE XIV.

REVENUE.

SECTION 1. The Grand Temple shall regulate the price of charters, warrants, rituals, constitutions, and blanks.

ARTICLE XV.

RULES OF ORDER.

SECTION 1. For rules of order, Dickson's Manual is hereby made the rule and guide.

ARTICLE XVI.

The Grand Temple can alter or amend this Constitution by proposing such alteration or amendment in open Grand Session, and if adopted by a two-thirds vote, the said alteration or amendment shall be submitted to the Temples and Tabernacles, in printed form, and if adopted by the majority vote of two-thirds of the Temples and Tabernacles, the next regular Grand Session shall, by a two-thirds vote, make such amendment or alteration a law.

REGULATIONS

OF THE

NATIONAL GRAND TEMPLE AND TABERNACLE.

ARTICLE I.

COMMITTEES.

SECTION 1. The C. G. M. shall, immediately after the opening of the Grand Session, appoint the following committees:

1. Committee on Credentials.
2. Committee on Returns of Temples.
3. Committee on Returns of Tabernacles.
4. Committee on C. G. M.'s Address and Report.
5. Committee on Ways and Means.
6. Committee on Complaints and Charges.
7. Committee on Appeals and Grievances.
8. Committee on C. G. S. and C. G. T.'s Report.
9. Committee on Obituaries.
10. Committee on the Condition of the Country.
11. Committee on Unfinished Business.
12. Committee on Printing Proceedings.

ARTICLE II.

DUTIES OF COMMITTEES.

Section 1. It shall be the duty of the Committee on Credentials to make out the roll of members of the Grand Temple, and to give the names of those that represent Temples and Tabernacles, and the names of proxy representatives for Temples and Tabernacles, or members.

Sec. 2. The Committee on Returns of Temples shall examine the annual returns, and report the number of members and the amount due to the Grand Temple.

Sec. 3. The Committee on Returns of Tabernacles shall examine the annual returns, and report the number of members and the amount due to the Grand Temple.

Sec. 4. The Committee on C. G. M.'s Address and Report shall examine it, and refer to proper committees, and make such recommendations and disposition of it as will best benefit the Order.

Sec. 5. The Committee on Ways and Means shall recommend to the Grand Temple the action to be taken on any matter that is referred to them.

Sec. 6. The Committee on Complaints and Charges shall examine all charges and complaints that come up to the Grand Temple, whether from

Temples or Tabernacles, or individual members, and report for the action of the Grand Temple.

SEC. 7. The Committee on Appeals and Grievances shall examine all appeals that come to the Grand Temple; have all the witnesses and evidence before them, make a decision, and submit it to the Grand Temple. Should the Grand Temple refuse, by a majority vote, to approve the action of the committee, a special committee of twelve shall be appointed by the Grand Temple to try the case. Their action shall be final. All grievances shall be referred and determined on by this committee, and reported to the Grand Temple.

SEC. 8. The Committee on C. G. S. and C. G. T.'s Report shall examine the annual reports of the two grand officers, audit them, and submit their action to the Grand Temple. They shall also review the accounts of the Board of Curators, and report. All accounts for money against the Grand Temple must be submitted to this committee, and reported on by them.

SEC. 9. The Committee on Obituaries shall examine the returns, and report the deaths of members of Temples and Tabernacles, with the proper obituaries and condolence.

SEC. 10. The Committee on the Country shall be appointed for one year. They will make up their report during the year, and report through their chairman at the annual session. It is their business to report the condition of the country, financially, educationally, socially, and otherwise.

Sec. 11. It shall be the duty of the Committee on Unfinished Business to report the business that was left by the last Grand Session unfinished, and report to the Grand Temple the nature of the business.

Sec. 12. The Committee on Printing shall have the transactions of the Grand Temple printed, and all other printed matter ordered by the Grand Temple. This committee shall be appointed for one year.

Sec. 13. All of the above committees shall consist of three members. The first named on the committee shall be the chairman.

Sec. 14. All other committees shall be called Special Committees, and shall be appointed by the C. G. M. or by the Grand Temple.

ARTICLE III.

RULES OF BUSINESS.

1. The Grand Temple shall meet on the constitutional day and hour, and open in the Temple Order, on the Sealed Daughters Degree.
2. The C. G. M. shall appoint the committees.
3. The address of the C. G. M.
4. Report of Committee on Credentials.

5. Report of Chief Grand Scribe.
6. Report of Chief Grand Treasurer.
7. Report of Board of Curators.
8. Reports of Standing Committees.
9. Reports of Special Committees.
10. Receive and refer and act upon Petitions, and New Business.
11. Nomination and election of officers.
12. Installation of officers.

ARTICLE IV.

REVENUE OF THE GRAND TEMPLE.

The revenue of the Grand Temple shall be received from the following sources:

1. Each member of a Temple shall pay to the Grand Temple, per year, ...
2. Members of the Tabernacle, per year, for each member, ...
3. Charter for Temple, etc., ...
4. Blanks (12) for new Temples, ...
5. Warrant for Tabernacle, etc., ...
6. Blanks for new Tabernacles, ...
7. Dispensations for Processions, Parades, or Festivals, ...
8. Dispensations (general), ...
9. Temple Constitutions, per dozen, ...
10. Tabernacle Constitutions, per dozen, . . .
11. Ritual and Lecture-Books, per dozen, . .
12. Blanks, per dozen, ...

ARTICLE V.

COMPENSATION PAY-ROLL.

SECTION 1. The salary of the C. G. M. and C. G. S. shall be fixed from time to time by the Grand Temple. The travelling expenses, at the rate of five cents per mile, shall be paid to the C. G. M., C. G. S., C. G. T., and such other officers as the Grand Temple may determine on at each annual session. The *per diem* of the above three officers shall be three dollars a day, during their attendance at the Grand Session.

SEC. 2. The Temples and Tabernacles shall pay the travelling expenses and *per diem* of the representatives to and from the Grand Temple Session.

ARTICLE VI.

TEMPLES AND TABERNACLES.

SECTION 1. It is the duty of every Temple and Tabernacle to send at least one delegate to the Grand Session. The Temple or Tabernacle that so far forgets or neglects this duty shall be dealt with by the action of the Grand Temple.

SEC. 2. A Temple or Tabernacle that neglects to pay their annual dues to the Grand Temple for two years shall, unless a satisfactory excuse be given and accepted by the Grand Temple, be suspended until all dues are paid.

SEC. 3. A proxy for a Temple or Tabernacle will

not be permitted to represent it until all dues are paid.

Sec. 4. A representative to the Grand Temple must be a Chief Mentor, Vice-Mentor, or Past Chief Mentor of a Temple, or a Chief Tribune of a Tabernacle, or Chief or Past Preceptress.

Sec. 5. Members and representatives must be clothed in proper regalia when in Grand Session.

ARTICLE VII.

THE MANNER OF GETTING A TEMPLE OR TABERNACLE.

Section 1. For the formation of a new Temple, a petition must be made to the C. G. M. by twelve Knights, with the full Temple Degree. Said petition will set forth the name of the city, county, and state, with certificates of withdrawal from the Temple or Temples to which they belonged.

Sec. 2. A new Tabernacle may be formed upon the petition of eight Daughters and three Knights to the C. G. M., their petition stating that they have the full Tabernacle Degrees, with said petition, the withdrawal certificates accompanying.

Sec. 3. In places where the Order is not established, it is not necessary for the applicants to petition in form, but apply to the C. G. M. or a D. G. M.

ARTICLE VIII.

CRIMES AND PENALTIES.

Section 1. Members of the Grand Temple may

be tried for violation of the laws, rules, and regulations of the Grand Temple; for immoral or improper conduct, and for criminal offences against the laws of the national government, state, county, city, and village.

SEC. 2. The penalty shall be named by the Committee on Charges and Complaints, after they have carefully heard all the testimony; and, when approved by the Grand Temple, it shall be final until revoked by action of the Grand Temple.

SEC. 3. All charges and complaints must be made in writing, and deposited with the C. G. S. or A. G. S., and read in open session, and referred to the proper committee.

Sec. 4. If the accused neglect or refuse to appear for trial when he is notified (without giving an acceptable excuse), he shall be declared guilty, and must abide the penalty.

ARTICLE IX.

BLANKS

SECTION 1. The C. G. S. shall furnish each Temple and Tabernacle with the following blanks:

Blank Annual Returns.

Blank Petitions for Membership.

Blank Travelling Certificates.

Blank Certificates of Withdrawal.

ARTICLE X.

REGALIA.

SECTION 1. C. G. M. — Pea-green velvet collar,

trimmed with gold fringe, with twelve yellow metal stars, with the emblematic figures, 777, on the right side; a rosette, pink color, with 333, metal; black navy cap, or chapeau, with green feather and appropriate trimmings, with gold bands, and metal letters T. D. P.; brown leather gloves, green gauntlets, with the emblematic star, and sword.

Sec. 2. P. C. G. M.—The same as the C. G. M., only with the addition of the letters P. G. M. on the left side of the collar.

Sec. 3. All other Grand Temple officers the same regalia, with this difference: wherever metal appears it must be white, and white silver fringe.

Sec. 4. Past officers wear the same, with the addition of the letters of their past office on the left side of the collar. The members' collars trimmed with silver fringe; seven silver stars; letters, on the right side, K. of T.; black navy cap, or chapeau, green feather, with appropriate trimming, with silver bands, and letters T. D. P.; brown leather gloves, green gauntlets, sword, etc.; belt, red patent-leather, two inches wide, metal clasp, with emblematic star; sword, white metal scabbard, cross handle,—sword to suit the height of the wearer.

REGALIA—SUBORDINATE TEMPLES.

Section 1. The color of the collar, light scarlet velvet, trimmed with silver lace and fringe; seven silver stars; blue navy cap, with silver bands, and white metal letters T. D. P.; brown gloves; gauntlets, dark scarlet, with emblematic star in silver; belt, red patent-leather, two inches wide, white metal clasp; sword, white metal or leather scabbard, tipped with metal, cross handle.

Sec. 2. The officers the same, with this addition: the initial of their office in metal letters on the side of the collar, the Past Officers with the initial "P" in addition to the other letters.

DRESS.

Sec. 3. The public dress shall be a black coat and black pants, coat buttoned up in front; black shoes or boots.

RECOMMENDATION.

Sec. 4. Care should be taken in the selection of the regalia, that all may get the proper color, and have them made after the regular pattern. For dress regalia get the best material. Let the caps and swords be all alike in your Temple. When you come out before the public have every thing clean and neat, but not gaudy.

WORKING REGALIA.

Sec. 5. The working regalia must be of the same color; it can be made of any material.

WHAT TO REMEMBER.

Sec. 6. Remember that our Order is not a copy of any other order, and that we are not copying after any other order; nor are we here for mere show; but we are organized for the substantial good and benefit of our members, and their widows and orphans; therefore, be careful what material you put in the Temple you are building, and do not make your Temple common by appearing often on parade. Take good care of your sick or disabled members, and bury your dead in a respectful manner. Obey every law, rule, and regulation; do your part to make your Temple a pleasant place to meet in. Be courteous and kind to all of the Order.

ARTICLE XI.

WIDOWS AND ORPHANS.

SECTION 1. The Grand Temple shall create a special fund, to be called the Widows and Orphans' Fund.

SEC. 2. This fund shall be managed by the Board of Grand Curators, and shall not be used for any other purpose but for the widows and orphans.

SEC. 3. The Grand Temple shall regulate the amount to be paid in monthly instalments to widows and orphans; this shall be done at each annual session.

SEC. 4. The Grand Temple shall define the manner, and through whom, the monthly instalment shall be paid.

Sec. 5. When a widow marries, the instalments must cease to be paid. Orphan instalments must be regulated by the Grand Temple.

Sec. 6. The Temple in whose jurisdiction the widow or orphans are must inform the Grand Temple of the condition of the family. Upon this report, the Grand Temple can determine the need of the instalment.

ARTICLE XII.

THE TEMPLE.

Section 1. A Temple must have their Charter framed and hung up in the Temple Hall. No Temple can be opened or any business done legally unless the Charter is present.

Sec. 2. All regular business must be done in the Third Degree. None but monthly business must be done at a stated meeting. All petitions must be acted on at this meeting.

Sec. 3. A special meeting must be called to give the degrees, or for lectures.

Sec. 4. The Constitution and Regulations must be read at a meeting called for that purpose, every three months, until the Temple is one year old; any explanation needed by the members at these readings shall be given by the C. M.

Sec. 5. A Temple can make their own by-laws or

regulations, but care must be taken that they do not conflict with the Constitution or the Regulations of the Grand Temple.

FURNITURE.

SEC. 6. The Temple House shall be three stories high: First story, eighteen inches square and one foot deep; second story, fifteen inches square and one foot deep; third story, ten inches square and one foot deep, made to open in each story. Color: First story, light scarlet; second story, pea-green; third story, white; moulding gilded. Lettering: First story — On one side, the name of the Temple and number; next side, the date of the organization; third side, the city and state; fourth side, Knights of Tabor, the Order of XII. Second story — First, 777; second, 999; third, 444; fourth, 333. Third story — First, the eye; second, the clasped hands; third, the ear; fourth, the emblematic star; rings and pole for carrying.

SEC. 7. The Book of Books; two cups; mallet; three pitchers; sword; girdle; star; shield; book of laws, and three candlesticks, staff and key.

EMBLEMS.

SEC. 8. The emblem can be made in any shape, with the emblematic 777 and the letters K. T. in plain view, or the emblematic letters, T. D. P.

PROCESSIONS.

Sec. 9. No Temple shall make a public display, except on funeral occasions, in any other month than August, without a dispensation.

Sec. 10. No Temple shall be named after any living man, except by order of the Grand Temple.

Sec. 11. No Sir Knight can be elected to the office of Chief Grand Mentor until he has served one year as Chief Mentor.

Sec. 12. A Past Chief Grand Mentor shall be an honorary member of the Temple to which he belongs, with all its rights, privileges, and benefits.

Sec. 13. Every Knight must be a member of a Temple, or he loses every right and privilege of the Order, and all its benefits.

ARTICLE XIII.

ORGANIZING NEW TEMPLES.

Section 1. The organization of Temples and Tabernacles is hereby vested in the Chief Grand Mentor, Past Grand Mentors, Vice-Grand Mentor, and Deputy Grand Mentors. These are the only legal officers to form organizations.

Sec. 2. The fee for organizing a new Temple, with fifteen or more members, shall not be less than $3 per member. For organizing with only the regular number (twelve), the fee shall not be less than $4 per member.

Sec. 3. The charter, books, blanks, and incorporation must be paid for out of the money received by the organizer.

Sec. 4. A chartered Temple shall not charge less than $5 for the degrees the first year of their organization. For the second year and thereafter, not less than $8 for the degrees.

Sec. 5. The price of charter, books, blanks, and incorporation shall be $18. No charter issued until the full amount is paid.

ARTICLE XIV.

NEW TABERNACLES.

Section 1. The fee for conferring the degrees and setting up a Ladies' Tabernacle, for any number more than twenty, shall be $2 each; for any number under twenty, the fee shall be $3 each.

Sec. 2. The price of warrant, books, blanks, and incorporation is hereby made $16. They must be paid for out of the money received by the organizer.

Sec. 3. A Ladies' Tabernacle shall not charge less than $3.50 for the degrees, during the first year of their organization; the second year and thereafter, the fee shall not be less than $5 for the degrees and membership.

ARTICLE XV.

LIFE POLICY.

SECTION 1. The life policy is for the benefit of the widow of a Knight of Tabor who has been a member of the Order in good standing for three consecutive years, or more.

SEC. 2. A special fund to perpetuate the policy is hereby created and set apart, said fund to be used for no other purpose.

SEC. 3. The National Grand Temple and Tabernacle shall make an annual assessment on each Sir Knight of not less than $1, the assessment to be paid at the annual session, with the Temple dues.

SEC. 4. The Grand Session shall, at the annual meeting, determine and fix the amount that is to be paid each widow. The Board of Curators will disburse the amount, under the orders of the Grand Temple and Tabernacle, and report to the Grand Session.

SEC. 5. The payment to be made annually at the Grand Session, and to continue during life and respectability, or until the widow marries.

ARTICLE XVI.

WIDOWS AND ORPHANS.

SECTION 1. A reserved fund is hereby set apart for the benefit of the widows and orphans; the widow, to receive this benefit for herself and children, must be a member in good standing in the Ladies' Tabernacle.

SEC. 2. The creation and perpetuation of this fund shall be as follows:

First—All money received into the Grand Temple and Tabernacle treasury, not otherwise appropriated, shall be paid into and become a part of this fund.

Second—Every Ladies' Tabernacle is hereby assessed $1 for every twelve members, annually, and 25 cents for every degree given each year. This money to be paid, with other dues, at the annual Grand Session.

SEC. 3. Every Temple shall pay into this fund 25 cents for each member, annually, with their other returns.

SEC. 4. The Board of Curators will disburse this money, under the orders of the Grand Temple and Tabernacle, and report to the annual Grand Session.

ARTICLE XVII.

HOW TO REPORT.

SECTION 1. The delegate to the Grand Temple and Tabernacle from a Temple, shall make a written statement, addressed to the Board of Curators, in detail, of the widows entitled to benefits under their Temple's jurisdiction, stating the age, condition, deportment, social standing, and residence of the widow.

Sec. 2. The representative to the Grand Session from a Ladies' Tabernacle must make a written report to the Board of Grand Curators, in detail, of the widows and orphans under the control of their Tabernacle, stating age, condition, and residence of the widow and children.

ARTICLE XVIII.

AMENDMENTS OR ALTERATIONS.

Section 1. To amend or alter any part of the Regulations of the Grand Temple, the amendment or alteration must be proposed in open session and read; and if received by a two-thirds vote, the said amendment or alteration shall be printed in the transactions, and be called up at the next session, and if adopted by a two-thirds vote of the Temple and Tabernacle delegates present, it shall become a law.

GRAND TEMPLE JEWELS.

(Gold, or Yellow Metal.)

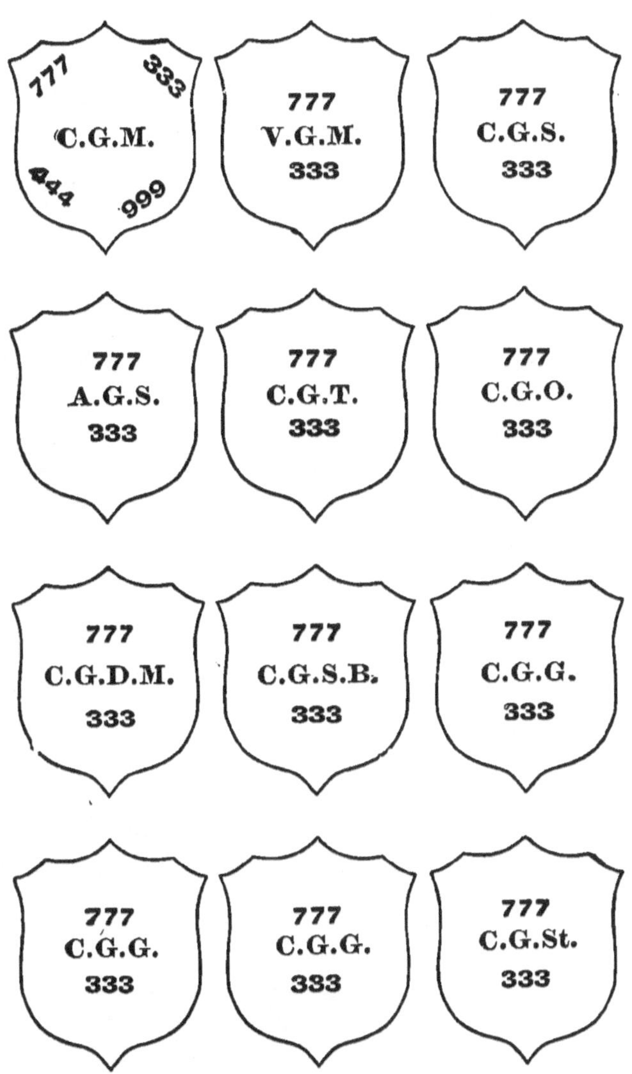

INSTALLATION CEREMONY.

The officers of the Temple can be installed in public or private. Any C. M., P. C. M., C. G. M., or P. C. G. M. have the authority to install.

INSTALLING THE OFFICERS OF THE GRAND TEMPLE.

When about to install, the installing officer will instruct the C. D. M., or the Marshal for the occasion, to conduct the officers elect to the anteroom. The installing officer takes his stand in front of the Temple House; the jewels of the officers will be placed upon it. The Knights are formed in line to the right and left in the hall, the right wing facing the left, — the centre of the hall clear. The C. G. D. M. marches the officers elect into the hall, and forms them in a semicircle, facing the Temple House, with the Grand Chief elect in the centre. The C. G. D. M. salutes the installing officer, and says:

Most faithful Grand Chief, it is with pleasure that I present to you these Sir Knights. They having been regularly elected to fill the several offices in the National Grand Temple for the ensuing term, they have signified their readiness to enter upon their official duties.

The installing officer then addresses the officers elect in these words:

Sir Knights, we are about to invest and intrust to your care the responsibility of carrying forward the work of the Knights of Tabor and the Daughters of the Tabernacle. The honor and stability of the Order of Twelve you are to guard with vigilance. It becomes my duty to administer to you the obligation that all Grand Officers have taken that have been installed. Are you willing to take it?

Answer. — We are willing to comply with the law and rules.

They place their right hands upon their breasts, and repeat after the installing officer the following

OATH OF OFFICE.

I, ——— ———, do solemnly promise and swear that I will support and defend the Constitution, Rules, and Regulations of the Grand Temple and Tabernacle of Knights of Tabor and Daughters of the Tabernacle of the United States of America. I will, with all my ability, faithfully attend to and do the duties of the office to which I have been elected.

The C. G. D. M. then places the Grand Chief elect in front of the Temple House, and says:

Most Faithful Grand Chief, I now present to you Sir ——— ———, who has been elected to the office of Chief Grand Mentor. He is now ready for installation.

The installing officer will then say:

Attention, Sir Knights. Return swords and doff caps. Let us bow our heads and unite in prayer with the Chief Grand Orator.

PRAYER.

Almighty God, who, through Thine only begotten Son, Jesus Christ, hast overcome death, and opened unto us the gate of everlasting life, we humbly beseech Thee that, as by Thy special grace helping us, Thou dost put into our minds good desires, so by Thy continual help we may bring the same to good effect.

O Lord, who never failest to help and govern those whom Thou dost bring up in Thy steadfast fear and love, keep us, we beseech Thee, under the protection of Thy good providence, and make us to have a perpetual fear and love of Thy holy name. We beseech Thee, O Lord, pour Thy grace into our hearts, that, as we have known the incarnation of Thy Son, Jesus Christ, by the message of an angel, so by His cross and passion we may be brought unto the glory of His resurrection.

In particular, we implore Thy grace and protection for the ensuing year. Keep us temperate in our meats and drinks, and diligent in our several callings. Grant us patience under any afflictions Thou shalt see fit to lay on us, and minds always contented with our present condition. Give us grace to be just and upright in all our dealings; quiet and peaceable, full of compassion, and ready to do good to all men, according to our abilities and opportunities. Direct us in all our ways, and prosper the works of our hands in the business of our several stations. Defend us from all dangers and adversities, and be graciously pleased to take us, and all things belonging to us, under Thy fatherly care and protection. These things, and whatever else Thou shalt see necessary and convenient to us, we humbly beg, through the merits and mediation of Thy Son, Jesus Christ, our Lord and Saviour. Amen.

Response. — Amen, amen, and amen!

The Sir Knights will cover, and the installing officer will proceed with the installation.

INSTRUCTION TO THE GRAND CHIEF ELECT.

Most Faithful Sir: You have been chosen by the suffrage of the Sir Knights to the most exalted position in the National Grand Temple. You have my congratulations upon your elevation to that eminent station. With pleasure I now invest you with the jewel of your office.

The C. G. D. M. affixes the badge to the left breast of the Grand Chief, and conducts him to the grand seat. The installing officer says:

Sir Knights, salute your Grand Chief.

The Sir Knights give the grand salute three times, and at each salute they say:

"We welcome!"

The installing officer then says:

Most Faithful Grand Chief: The evident love you have for our beloved Order, and your intimate acquaintance with the duties of every department to work the laws, rules, and regulations of the Temple and Tabernacle, makes it unnecessary that I should repeat them at this time. The high honor of this office has its weighty responsibilities. Your authority will be respected by every true Knight; your commands and orders will meet with ready obedience. Each Taborian Knight will cheerfully sustain you in your care over the interests of your large jurisdiction. You will feel the necessity in your daily life and actions to exemplify the excellent teachings of our beloved Order. Be thou an example that all Sir Knights will gladly follow. Be faithful to the end.

The installing officer says to the Grand Temple:

"Behold your Grand Chief."

The Grand Temple is seated; and if the Grand Chief desires to make any remarks, this is the proper time.

When the Grand Chief closes his remarks, the G. C. D. M. presents the other grand officers for installation, which can be done by the Grand Chief in person, or by deputy.

INSTRUCTION TO THE VICE-GRAND MENTOR.

Right Faithful Sir: The important station to

which the suffrages of your brother Knights have called you demonstrates the confidence that they have in your integrity and ability, and that you will faithfully discharge the duties of the office. You are the nearest successor of the Chief Grand Mentor. Should any unforeseen casualty happen to him, so as to prevent him from fulfilling the duties committed to his care, which the Lord forbid, you are to assume the responsibilities and functions of that office. In his presence, you are to assist him with counsel and advice. I now invest you with the jewel of your office. Be faithful to duty.

INSTRUCTION TO THE CHIEF SCRIBE.

Right Faithful Sir: The useful and honorable station that the voice of your brother Knights has called you to fill shows the confidence they repose in your capacity to discharge the duties of this most important office. The position is one that requires prompt action and punctuality, and a strict fidelity to matters and business appertaining to your several duties. I have no doubt but that you will use all diligence and correctness in the discharge of the important duties committed to your care, that benefit may accrue to the Grand Temple and Tabernacle, and honor be awarded to you by the Sir Knights. I now invest you with the jewel of your office. Be faithful to your duty.

INSTRUCTION TO THE ASSISTANT GRAND SCRIBE.

Right Faithful Sir: You have been elected to the duties of Assistant Grand Scribe by the will of your brother Knights. Every station in the Grand

Temple and Tabernacle is an honor to him that receives it. Be true to your Order and faithful to your promise. I now invest you with the jewel of your office. Remember the books.

INSTRUCTION TO THE CHIEF GRAND TREASURER.

Right Faithful Sir: The members of the Grand Temple and Tabernacle, in their choice of you to the very responsible station of Grand Treasurer, have proved the confidence they have in your integrity and honor. The qualities that should be found in the officer that fills this position are honesty, accuracy, and faithfulness. Be accurate in keeping a fair account of all receipts and disbursements, and careful in preserving all the property and moneys that may come into your hands with fidelity; render a just account of all your business with the Order, when called on by the proper authority. I now invest you with the jewel of your office. Be faithful and prompt in the discharge of the trust we now confide to your hands.

INSTRUCTION TO THE CHIEF GRAND ORATOR.

Right Faithful Sir: Reverend brother Knight, your high calling as a Christian minister has prepared you for the duties to which you have been elected. Your official duty is of the highest importance to Sir Knights, and so interesting that they require punctual attendance at all meetings of the Grand Temple and Tabernacle. May you be thoroughly furnished and abundantly provided for the good work. May you be established and perfected in your holy order by Him who presides and rules over the destinies of mankind, and sits as Supreme Grand Chief of the Universe. I now invest you with the jewel of your office. Be thou faithful until your work is finished on earth, and the Most Faithful Grand Chief of the Heavenly Temple will give you a crown of life.

INSTRUCTION TO THE CHIEF GRAND DRILL-MASTER.

Right Faithful Sir: Having been elected to the important station of Chief Grand Drill-Master, you will find pleasure in the discharge of your several duties. I admonish you to be zealous and active in your teachings and instructions to the Sir Knights. You have in charge the entrance of the Grand Temple and Tabernacle during the hours of business, and the command of the Sir Knights when on duty. I would remind you of the necessity of diligence in the duties that devolve upon you. I now invest you with the jewel of your office. Be thou a faithful soldier, and promptly discharge every duty.

INSTRUCTION TO THE CHIEF STANDARD-BEARER.

Right Faithful Sir: To you has been intrusted the banner of our Order. The distinguished honor of being Grand Standard-Bearer of the Knights of Tabor having been conferred on you by the voice of your brother members, I now give to your care and official custody the *gonfalon* of the Grand Temple. It is the rallying-point in time of danger. It is your duty to display and protect it when it is unfurled. It reminds the Sir Knights that our order is perpetuated for the benefit and good of humanity. I now invest you with the jewel of your office. Be faithful to the trust we give into your hands. May the Lord give you strength.

INSTRUCTION TO THE CHIEF GRAND GUARDS.

Right Faithful Sirs: Having been elected to the station of Chief Grand Guards, I congratulate you upon the trust that is reposed in your worthiness to attend the important duties pertaining to your office. You will, therefore, be punctual in the observance of the several official duties of the station, by which you will merit the approval of your brother members, and the honorable commendation of all Sir Knights. I now invest you with the jewel of your office. Be faithful to every duty.

INSTRUCTION TO THE CHIEF GRAND SENTINEL.

Right Faithful Sir: The responsibility of the station to which you have been elected by the suffrage of your brother Knights — that of Chief Grand Sentinel — cannot be estimated. Holding the outpost and guarding the entrance of our sacred Temple, I admonish you to be vigilant and sleepless. Look well to every avenue of approach. May you have courage to keep every enemy at bay. Be kind and courteous to all Sir Knights that hail the outer portals. I now invest you with the jewel of your office. Be thou faithful as a watchman upon the outer lines, and give timely warning of any approaching danger.

INSTRUCTION TO THE BOARD OF GRAND CURATORS.

Sir Knights: By the will of your brother Knights, you have been called to the duties of Grand Curators. The position is of great responsibility and sacred trust. To you are intrusted the funds of the widows and orphans of deceased Sir Knights. The gifts and donations for the benefit of the Grand Temple or subordinate Temples and Tabernacles are placed in your charge. I need not admonish you to be watchful of the interests of our Order, for you would not have been chosen had not the members of the Grand Temple and Tabernacle had the utmost confidence in your integrity and ability. I now invest you with the jewel of your office. Be ye faithful, and let your light shine with true goodness. Be zealous in the discharge of every known duty.

THE OFFICERS OF THE GRAND TABERNACLE.

The Most Faithful Chief Grand Mentor announces the appointments made for the Grand Tabernacle. As each name is announced, the Chief Grand Drill-Master conducts the Daughter to her appropriate seat, and proclaims her name and office. The Sir Knights that are not in office stand during this part of the ceremony. After which all are seated, and the Past Chief Grand Mentor or the Chief Grand Orator delivers the following charge:

CHARGE TO GRAND OFFICERS.

Sir Knights: Having been elected and installed,

with the necessary ceremonies, into the several stations of the Grand Temple and Tabernacle, the duties of your various positions you will find fully laid down in the Constitutions of the Order. While your work seems separate and divided, it is really not so. In the erection of our Temple a variety of material is used. Workmen of separate callings have their part to perform to make the building complete. Just so we are building a great Temple for the good and interest of humanity. The erection requires sundry talents and various workmen, each in their several departments. Collectively and individually, you are to contribute your part in the grand undertaking, that, by a union of action and a determination to do your whole duty, our Order will continue to move forward to power and usefulness. The past history of the Grand Temple and Tabernacle is a gallant one. Its record is clear and bright. That you will earnestly strive to keep it so I have no doubt. I ask you to put your trust in the Lord of Hosts. He is a tower of strength. By the faithful discharge of your several duties, you will receive the hearty approval of your brother members. May God, the giver of every good and perfect gift, guide and direct you in your labor of love. Take the shield of faith and the sword of the spirit, and the breast-plate of righteousness, which is the command of God. May peace and harmony, and faith in the Lord Jesus Christ, be with you all forever. Amen.

Response.—May the Lord direct us.

THE REVIEW.

The procession is formed of Sir Knights and Daughters, and marched three times around the hall. The officers remain seated. When the Daughters are seated, the Knights are exercised in the sword drill by the Chief Grand Drill-Master.

Yours Truly
Amos Johnson

Elected and installed Chief Grand Mentor at the Annual Session, August, A.D. 1878.

KNIGHT EMBLEMS.

(Gold or Silver.)

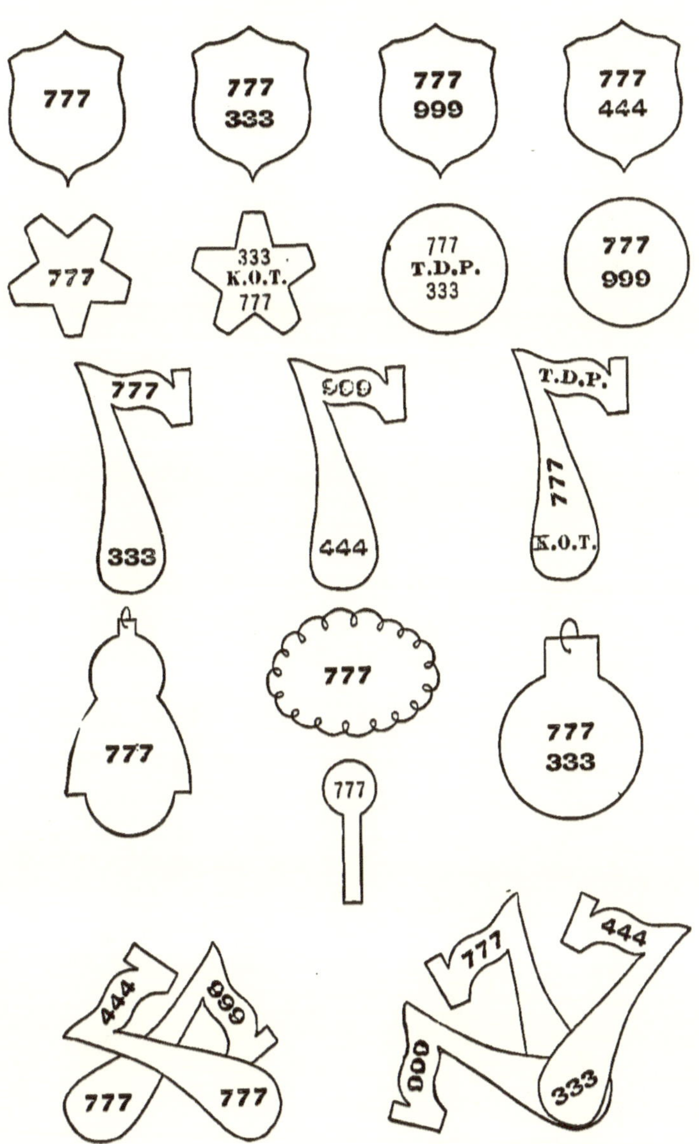

GRAND TEMPLE AND TABERNACLE.

1. The Grand Temple will open for business in the Sealed Daughters Degree.

2. The officers are seated as the form represents.

3. The Ladies' Tabernacle is represented in the Grand Temple by the Chief Preceptress or the Tribunes.

4. The Grand Officers of the Tabernacle are appointed by the Chief Grand Mentor immediately after his installation. They hold an honorary position, — an office of honor.

5. The Chief Grand Preceptress is seated to the left of the C. G. M.

6. The Vice-Grand Preceptress is seated to the left of the V. G. M.

7. The Chief Grand Recorder is seated to the left of the C. G. S.

8. The Vice-Grand Recorder is seated to the left of the A. G. S.

9. The Chief Grand Treasurer is seated to the left of the C. G. T.

10. The Chief Grand Priestess is seated to the left of the C. G. O.

11. The Chief Grand Inner Sentinel is seated to the right of the C. G. D. M.

12. The Chief Grand Outer Sentinel is seated to the left of the I. G. S.

13. The Board of Grand Visitors are seated to the left of the Board of Grand Curators.

14. The Board of Grand Examiners are seated to the left of the C. G. T.

15. Past Grand Mentors and Past Grand Preceptresses are seated to the right of the C. G. M.

16. The letter "D" is where the C. G. D. M. stands when he proclaims the installation of the Daughters.

17. The officers, members, and visitors must wear their appropriate regalia and jewels during the session of the Grand Temple.

18. The Sir Knights have seventeen Grand Officers, the Ladies' Tabernacle have fourteen Grand Officers in the Grand Temple, making a total of thirty-one Grand Officers.

19. A Sir Knight that has been installed Chief Mentor is a life-member of the Grand Temple.

20. The Vice-Mentor is a member of the Grand Temple during his term of office.

21. A Daughter that has been installed a Chief Preceptress is a life-member of the Grand Temple.

22. The Tribunes of the Ladies' Tabernacle are members of the Grand Temple during their term of office.

23. When a member of the Grand Temple loses his or her membership in a Subordinate Temple or Tabernacle, they lose their membership in the Grand Temple also.

24. The members of the Grand Temple, to perpetuate their membership, are required to pay $1 per year into the Widows and Orphans' Fund.

25. A neglect to pay the Grand Temple fee of $1 for two consecutive years will work a forfeiture of membership.

26. All visitors to the Grand Temple must be in good standing in their Temple or Tabernacle.

FORM OF TEMPLE.

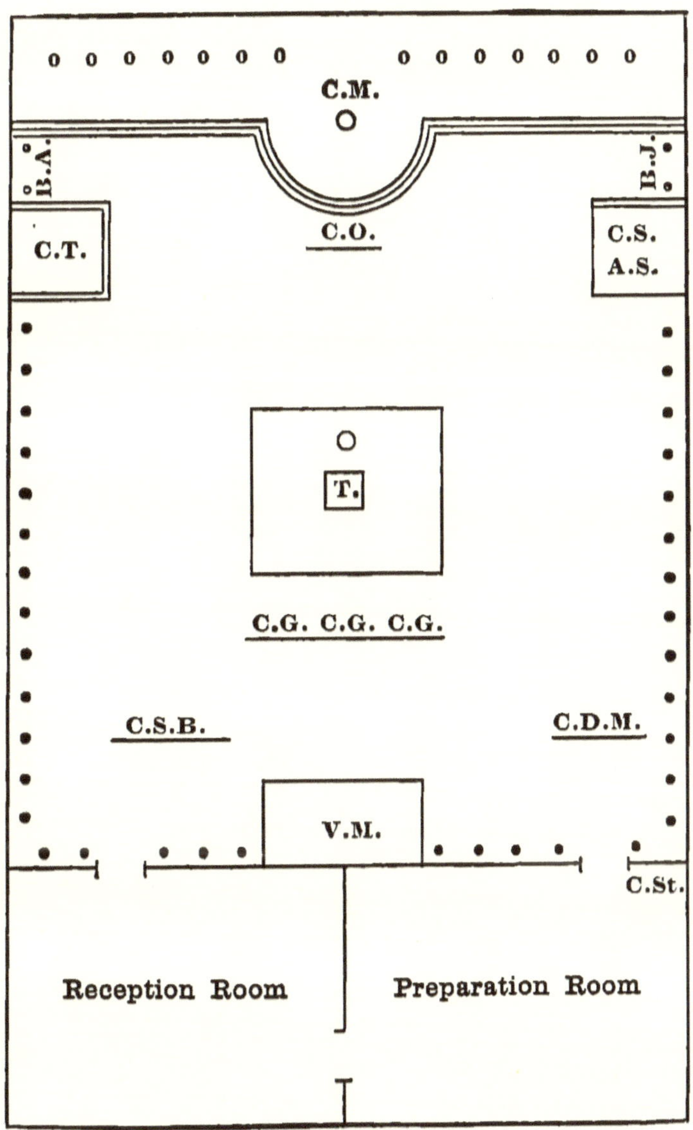

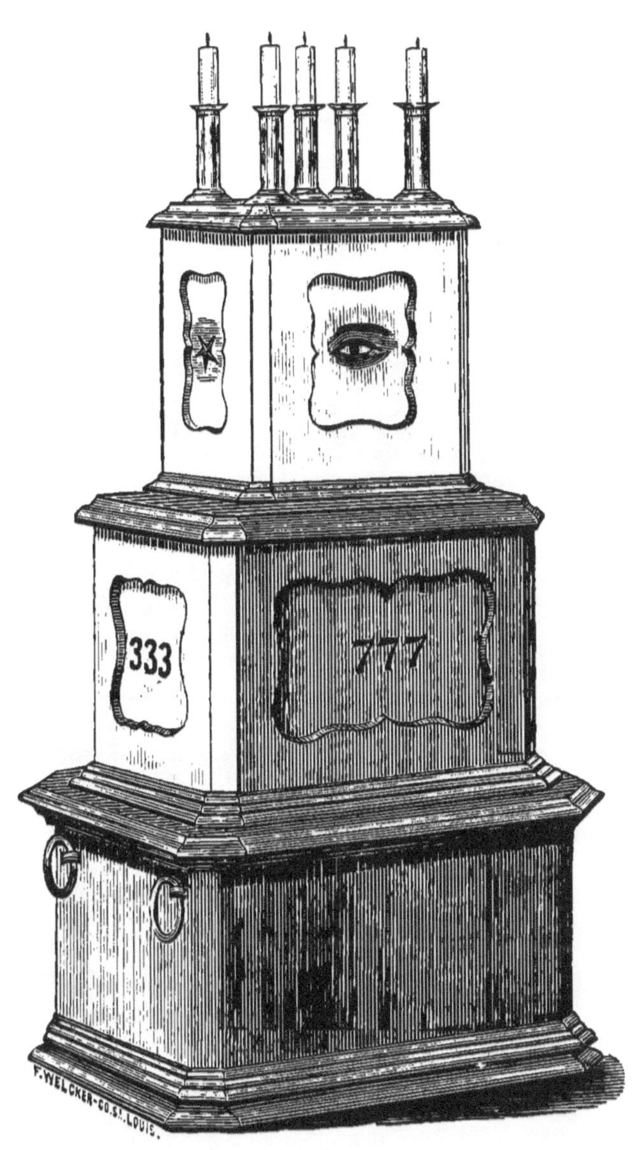

FORM OF TEMPLE HOUSE.

CONSTITUTION,

RULES AND REGULATIONS

OF

SUBORDINATE TEMPLES

OF

KNIGHTS OF TABOR.

CONSTITUTION

OF

SUBORDINATE TEMPLES.

ARTICLE I.

SECTION 1. This Temple shall be known by name as the ———, No. —, of ———, State of ———, of the Knights of Tabor, and not otherwise.

SEC. 2. The officers shall be:

1. A Chief Mentor, ... C. M.
2. A Vice-Mentor, ... V. M.
3. A Chief Scribe, ... C. S.
4. Assistant Scribe, ... A. S.
5. Chief Treasurer, ... C. T.
6. Chief Orator, ... C. O.
7. Chief Drill-Master, ... C. D. M.
8. Chief Standard-Bearer, ... C. S. B.
9. Chief Guard, ... C. G.
10. Chief Guard, ... C. G.
11. Chief Guard, ... C. G.
12. Chief Sentinel, ... C. St.

Sec. 3. All of them shall be elected annually, at the regular meeting in the month of July, and installed on or before the second Tuesday in the month of August of each year.

ARTICLE II.

THE DUTIES OF OFFICERS.

Section 1. It shall be the duty of the Chief Mentor to preside at all the meetings of the Temple. He shall call special meetings whenever he may deem it necessary. He shall decide all questions of law, order, or rules. The Temple, whenever in session, shall be under his supervision, and he shall cause the business to be done by the rules. He shall decide the time for closing, without a motion. He shall perform all other duties belonging to his office.

VICE-MENTOR.

Sec. 2. The V. M. shall fill the duties of the C. M. when he is absent, and, in his presence, assist in the several duties of the office. Should both C. M. and V. M. be absent at the hour of opening meetings, one of the Chief Guards opens the Temple and fills the duties of the presiding officer *pro tem.*

CHIEF SCRIBE.

Sec. 3. The Chief Scribe shall keep the books of the Temple, — the records and the roll of members. He shall keep a regular account with each member, and collect all dues, fines, and other moneys belonging to the Temple, and pay them into the treasury. He shall record the doings of each meeting plainly and neatly, and report to the Temple, when called on, the condition of the treasury. He shall make a regular report of the Temple, at the regular meeting in the month of July. He shall draw all orders for money on the treasury, and see that they are signed by the C. M., and countersigned by himself.

ASSISTANT SCRIBE.

Sec. 4. It shall be the duty of the Assistant Scribe to assist the C. S. in his several duties, and to fulfil all the duties of the C. S. when he, the C. S., is absent.

CHIEF TREASURER.

Sec. 5. The Chief Treasurer shall receive all the moneys and valuables belonging to the Temple, and pay all orders when drawn properly. He shall keep a correct account of all moneys received and paid out. He shall report, when called on by the C. M., the condition of the treasury. He shall make a report at the regular meeting in July. He shall give a bond, to secure the money of the Temple, to the C. M., C. O., and C. T., for the faithful application of the Temple's money, per Constitution, — the amount of the bond to be agreed on at a regular meeting of the Temple. He shall give to his successor a written statement of the treasury. He shall, when his successor is qualified, turn over to him all books, cash, papers, and other property that is in his possession.

CHIEF ORATOR.

Sec. 6. The Chief Orator shall conduct the devotional exercises of the Temple, and visit and give consolation to the sick and disabled members. He shall attend the funeral exercises of Sir Knights and Daughters.

CHIEF DRILL-MASTER.

Sec. 7. It shall be the duty of the C. D. M. to teach the members the march and drill. He shall teach the sword-exercise, and assist in giving the degrees. He shall attend the inner door of the Temple, and shall be Marshal on all public occasions.

CHIEF STANDARD-BEARER.

Sec. 8. It shall be the duty of the C. S. B. to carry the banner of the Order, and keep it in his possession, — to preserve and keep it ready for use.

CHIEF GUARDS.

Sec. 9. The Chief Guards shall assist the C. M. in giving the degrees, and in preserving order during the hours of business.

CHIEF SENTINEL.

Sec. 10. It shall be the duty of the Chief Sentinel to guard the outside door of the Temple, under the order of the C. M. He shall prepare and keep the Temple in proper order for the meetings. He shall receive such compensation as may be awarded by the Temple for his services.

BOARD OF ATTENDANTS.

SEC. 11. This Board shall consist of three members, who shall be appointed by the C. M. on the night of his installation. It shall be the duty of the Board to have oversight of all the members of the Temple, and report to the C. M. when a member is sick or disabled, and what attendance the member needs. This Board shall draw and pay the sick dues; they shall notify, by order of the C. M., members who are detailed to sit up with sick or disabled members. This Board shall arrange and prepare the funeral of a deceased Knight.

SEC. 12. This Board shall have the oversight of Sir Knights' widows and orphans, and report their condition to the Temple at every regular meeting.

SEC. 13. This Board shall keep a book and record their doings, and it shall be their duty to report to the Temple at the regular monthly meeting what they have done during the month.

BOARD OF JUDGES.

SEC. 14. This Board shall consist of five members, who shall be appointed by the C. M. on the night he is installed. To this Board shall be referred all matters of difference between members, and all trials of members for any offence whatever.

Sec. 15. This Board shall hold regular meetings, and shall have the power to summon witnesses and the plaintiff and defendant, and carefully hear all sides, make up their decision, and report to the Temple, through their Secretary. The Temple shall enforce their recommendation, and their action shall be final when approved by the Temple.

Sec. 16. This Board shall audit the accounts of the C. S. and C. T., and report to the Temple at the regular meeting in the month of July.

Sec. 17. This Board shall have a book, and keep a record of their doings. The Secretary of the Board shall read their report at every regular meeting.

ARTICLE III.

MEMBERSHIP.

Section 1. Any man of moral habits and sound health, respected in the community that he lives in, and a believer in God, age not less than nineteen years, may apply for membership by petition.

Sec. 2. Any member can receive and bring a petition to the Temple. A petition must be accompanied with the fee, and state the age and residence of the petitioner.

BALLOT.

Sec. 3. Petitions for membership must be read

at a stated meeting. If the petitioner is well known, the ballot must be had at that meeting; if he is not, the Chief Mentor shall appoint a special committee to report on his qualification at the next stated meeting.

Sec. 4. The ballots must be black and white balls. If three or more black balls appear in the ballot-box, the candidate shall be rejected. He can apply again in three months.

Sec. 5. The ballot-box must have two apartments, with a substantial cover, with a hole in the cover, for secret ballot.

ARTICLE IV.

THE MEETINGS.

Section 1. There shall be one stated or regular meeting of the Temple in each month; the time shall be fixed in the regulations of the Temple. Nothing but the monthly business can be done at a stated meeting, and the Temple must be opened in the Third Degree.

Sec. 2. The C. M. can call a special meeting at any time for the giving of degrees, lectures, drills, trials, or any matter other than the monthly business.

Sec. 3. All meetings must open at the hour named in the regulations. Officers and members must be present within thirty minutes after the Temple is opened, or pay such fines as are assessed by the regulations.

ARTICLE V.

FEES AND DUES.

SECTION 1. The fee for giving the degrees shall be named in the Temple's regulations. For a travelling certificate, $1; members from other Temples wishing to enroll their names and become members, $1.

SEC. 2. The C. S. shall collect from the new-made member, before his name is enrolled, $1 for the Widows and Orphans' Fund.

SEC. 3. The Chief Mentor shall have power to tax the members, in equal proportion, to raise any needed amount of money for the Temple.

SEC. 4. The monthly dues must be named in the Temple's regulations.

SEC. 5. At the next stated meeting after the death and burial of a member, every member shall pay into the treasury of the Temple $1.

ARTICLE VI.

BENEFITS.

SECTION 1. Every member who has received the Third Degree, with the key, shall be a beneficial member, entitled to receive, when sick or disabled so as to prevent them from attending their usual business, weekly benefits, as prescribed by the regulations of the Temple.

SEC. 2. A sick or disabled member who is out of

the jurisdiction can receive his weekly benefits by sending his application to the C. S., with a certificate from the attending physician, stating the time he has been in attendance and the nature of the disease, with such other proof as may be required by the Temple.

Sec. 3. A Sir Knight being sick or disabled in the jurisdiction of another Temple, can apply to that Temple for the weekly benefit, and receive it, provided he can furnish acceptable proof that he is in good standing at home. The Temple that pays the sojourner's benefit must give notice to the Temple the sojourner belongs to, and draw from that Temple the amount disbursed for its member.

Sec. 4. Not more than four weeks' benefit shall be paid, on applications of sections 2 and 3, at one time; that is, if the member is sick or disabled a longer time than four weeks, orders for money must be sent to his Temple every four weeks.

Sec. 5. On the death of a member, the Temple shall bury him (unless his family object) in a respectable manner, worthy of the Order of Knighthood. The Temple shall not go into any extravagant expense in a funeral.

Sec. 6. When a member dies outside of his jurisdiction, the nearest Temple shall attend to all the burial arrangements, and draw on his Temple for the expenses; or, should the Temple to which the deceased member belonged desire his remains to be sent home, the Temple in whose jurisdiction he died shall attend to the request, and draw on his Temple for the expense.

SEC. 7. On the death of a Sir Knight who has been a member of the Temple in good standing for the time fixed by the Grand Temple, and who is not in arrears for dues or fines at the time of his decease, his widow shall receive, from the Life Fund, the regular annual allowance; the benefits to continue as long as the Board of Attendants decide that it is needed, under the regulations of the Temple.

SEC. 8. When a sick or disabled member needs the attendance of the Knights at his bedside, the C. M. shall detail one or more brother Knights to sit up with him. The C. M. shall commence the detail from the bottom of the roll and up, until all have taken their turn.

ARTICLE VII.

THE TEMPLE.

SECTION 1. The meeting-place of the Temple must be secure from prying eyes, and where the business will not be exposed.

SEC. 2. The Temple must have a seal, with the name and number. The impress of the seal must be made on all the official papers.

SEC. 3. The Temple can make their own regulations; these shall have the power of by-laws, when not in conflict with the Constitution.

SEC. 4. The Temple can try, and suspend or expel its members for any offence against constitutional law or regulations, or for any criminal offence against common law.

SEC. 5. No Temple shall make public display (except in the month of August, or for funeral occasions) without obtaining a dispensation from the C. G. M.

SEC. 6. Any Temple that causes to be printed any of the private work of the Temple shall, on proof of the same, forfeit its charter.

SEC. 7. A Temple cannot try its C. M. or V. M. for any offence; they can only be tried by the Grand Temple.

SEC. 8. The Temple must be furnished neat and plain, with all the necessary appliances to conduct the work properly.

ARTICLE VIII.

DUTIES OF MEMBERS.

SECTION 1. It shall be the duty of every member to be present and assist in the business of every session of the Temple.

SEC. 2. A member must attend, in regular order, to the comforts and needs of a sick or disabled Sir Knight, when notified by the presiding officer.

Sec. 3. Members must be true to the interests of the Temple, and cultivate a friendly feeling toward Sir Knights; live in peace and harmony, and protect the interests and good name of every member.

Sec. 4. That the business and expenses of the Temple may be kept in a good condition, and be a benefit to all the members, it is the imperative duty of every member to pay his dues and assessments punctually and regularly.

Sec. 5. It is the duty of a Sir Knight, when about to go on a journey, to take a travelling-certificate, as an evidence of his good standing.

Sec. 6. It is the duty of every member to aid and support the officers in doing their duty; be a prop and stay in every thing for the benefit and good name of the Temple.

ARTICLE IX.

BENEFITS AND RIGHTS.

First. — Every Knight shall have the right to visit and meet in his own Temple, and any other Temple or Tabernacle.

Second. — He shall have the right to participate and take part in any public display of his own Temple, or any other Temple or Tabernacle.

Third. — It is the right of a Knight to receive, when sick or disabled so as to prevent him from following his usual business, the weekly benefit, and the attendance of the brother Knights; when poor and in distress, and needy, to receive aid and comfort from any brother Knight.

Fourth. — It is his right to travel with a certificate of good standing.

Fifth. — It is his right to receive an honorable interment by the members of his own Temple, and have his widow and orphans cared for.

Sixth. — The above rights and benefits are only given to Sir Knights who are in good standing.

ARTICLE X.

A FORFEITURE OF BENEFITS AND RIGHTS.

Section 1. When a member is three months in arrears for dues, or fails to pay his fines or taxes within thirty days after they are assessed, unless excused by a vote of the Temple, the C. S. shall announce the name of the member at any stated meeting, stating the amount due. If the said member (or members) fail to pay within thirty days after this notice, he shall stand suspended until all dues, fines, and taxes are paid.

Sec. 2. A member who is suspended forfeits his right to all the benefits of the Temple until he is restored.

Sec. 3. A member who is expelled is dead to all the rights and benefits of the Temple, and forfeits every right belonging to a Knight. The only way he can be restored is at a stated meeting, by a resolution adopted by two-thirds of the members of the Temple. If he is expelled a second time, he cannot be restored.

ARTICLE XI.

CRIMES AND PENALTIES.

SECTION 1. Members of the Temple may be tried for violation of laws, regulations, and rules of the Temple; for immoral conduct, improper language, criminal offences against the laws, the national, state, county, or city government.

SEC. 2. All trials shall be had before the judges. After they have carefully heard all the testimony, they can make their report, guilty or not guilty, to a stated meeting of the Temple; if approved by a majority vote of the Temple, the penalty shall be assessed by the Temple, and the member must abide the penalty. He can appeal to the Grand Temple by giving notice immediately.

SEC. 3. All charges and complaints must be made in writing to the C. S., stating the nature of the charges, and giving the names of two or more witnesses. The C. S. will read it at a stated meeting. The C. M. will refer it to the judges.

SEC. 4. If the accused refuse or neglect to appear for trial after he is notified, without giving a reasonable excuse, he shall be declared guilty, and stand the penalty.

SEC. 5. Should one or more of the judges be the

party accused, the C. M. shall appoint others to fill their places during the trial.

SEC. 6. If the C. M. and V. M. should in any manner so far forget their positions as leaders and examples for other members to copy after, and commit crimes, or violate the laws, regulations, or rules of the Order, the members can meet and make a written complaint to the C. G. M. The complaint must be signed by two-thirds of the members. When such complaint is made, it is the duty of the C. G. M. to call the C. M.'s, or the P. C. M.'s, of three different Temples to go and investigate the case; and, if they find the party guilty of an offence that will injure the good name of the Temple, they shall suspend him until the session of the Grand Temple; or, their report can clear him. In all cases, they must give notice of their action to the C. G. M.

SEC. 7. It is not the intention of the founders of the Temple, in giving a code of laws, to compel Sir Knights to do their duty; that is made plain by their obligation, constitutions, regulations, and rules. A Sir Knight who will not do his plain duty without being compelled, is not fit to remain a member of the Temple. Try him two or three times. If he is contentious, quarrelsome, creating confusion; will not attend regularly to the meetings; lets his dues and assesments run over the time; always fault-finding, and is not a gentleman in deportment, conversation, and manners, *expel him, and warn all other Temples. Be sure and receive him no more.*

ARTICLE XII.

FUNERALS.

SECTION 1. It is the duty of every Sir Knight to attend and assist at the funerals of Sir Knights and Daughters.

SEC. 2. The dress is the regulation dress; the regalia, sword, cap, gloves, and gauntlets, to be worn at a Sir Knight's funeral.

SEC. 3. At a Daughter's funeral, the regulation dress, with collar, cap, and white gloves.

SEC. 4. The regulation dress is black coat, black pants, and black boots or shoes, the coat buttoned up in front.

ARTICLE XIII.

THE DEGREES.

The degrees shall be known by Title: First — The Title. Second — The Lock. Third — The Key Knight. The Knights receive the Daughters' degrees in addition to their regular degrees.

ARTICLE XIV.

RULES OF ORDER.

1. The presiding officer, at the proper hour, takes his seat and gives one rap; the officers and members

clothe in regalia and take their respective seats. The Temple is then opened in order.

2. The regular business of the Temple shall be done without a motion, as it is prescribed in the Rules of Business.

3. During the reading of the minutes, communications, or other papers, silence shall be observed. After they are read, the minutes, if they are correct, stand approved; if there is a question of their correctness, the member who questions their correctness shall state what is not correct, and move that the correction be made.

4. Members and visitors must come to the hall cleanly dressed, wearing the working regalia and white gloves.

5. A member, when addressing the Temple, shall stand, and address the C. M. as Sir Chief.

6. During the time that the Temple is open and doing business, no refreshments, smoking or chewing tobacco will be permitted.

7. When a C. G. M. or a P. C. G. M. visits the Temple, he must be received with the standing grand honors.

8. When a Grand Officer visits the Temple, he must be received standing.

9. All officers in open Temple shall be addressed by the title of their office, all members as Sir Knight; these titles only to be used in open Temple, or when on duty or parade.

10. When it is necessary to get the sense of the Temple on any question or resolution, it must be done by motion and second, and stated by the presiding officer, and decided by the voting sign.

11. When an officer is absent from a meeting of the Temple, the C. M. can appoint a member to fill the office *pro tem.*

12. When an office is made vacant by death, resignation, or for any other cause, the C. M. shall appoint a member to fulfil the duties until the regular election.

13. The C. M. shall control the business of the Temple, and determine the time to close, without a motion.

14. The regular business of the Temple shall be done by the Rules of Business.

15. The C. M. shall be responsible to the Grand Temple for the manner in which he administers the laws of the Temple. He shall decide all doubtful questions of constitution, regulations, and order. His decision shall be final until reversed by the C. G. M. or the Grand Temple.

16. No member shall speak more than once on the same subject, until all who wish to speak have spoken; nor more than twice, without permission from the C. M. No member shall speak longer than ten minutes.

RULES OF BUSINESS.

1. Opening at the proper hour.

2. Reading the proceedings of the last regular and intervening meetings; correcting and adopting.

3. Reports of the Boards read and adopted.

4. Receiving and reading petitions for the degrees or membership.

5. Balloting on petitions.

6. Calling the roll and collecting dues and fines, taxes, etc.

7. Unfinished business.

8. New business, motions, and resolutions.

9. Report of the C. S. and C. T., every three months.

10. News from other Temples or Tabernacles.

11. The C. M.'s charge to the members.

12. Closing the Temple.

FORM OF A PETITION.

The undersigned, believing the Knights of Tabor a good institution, wishes to become a member, and asks to be accepted. Age, . . . Residence, ... Occupation, ... Enclosed fee, $ . . . Dated, ... 18 . .

Signed, ...

FORM OF CERTIFICATE.

This is to certify that the bearer, ... is a member of the Knights of Tabor, in good standing, and this certificate was granted by . . . . Temple No. . . . . of the city of . . . . county of . . . . . . State of . . . . . . this . . . day of . . . . . . A. D. . . . .

Signed, ... C. S.

{ SEAL }

. . . . C. M.

FORM OF TRANSFER.

This is to certify that the bearer, ... was a member in good standing of . . . . . . Temple, No. . . . . of . . . . of the Knights of Tabor. He is hereby permitted to enroll in any Temple, provided not more than sixty days elapse after date of this transfer.

Dated, ... 18 . .

{ SEAL } Signed, ... C. M.

Attested, ... C. S.

THE MANUAL.

For a book of Ceremonies, Drill, and Practice, get "Dickson's Manual of the Temple and Tabernacle."

777 — 999 — 444 — 333 — T. D. P.

TEMPLE JEWELS.

(Silver.)

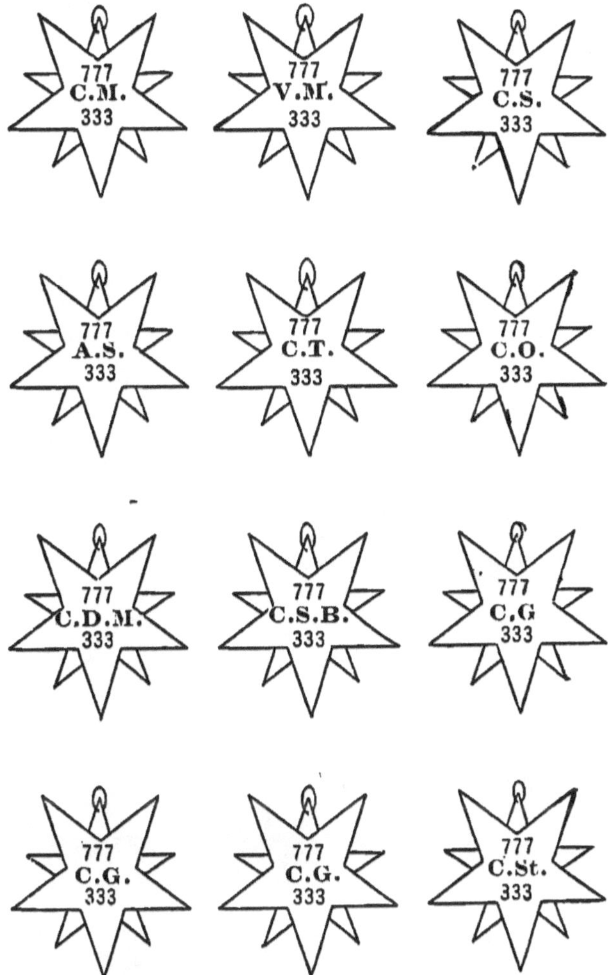

INSTALLATION CEREMONY.

The installation of the officers of a Temple can be performed either in public or private. Any C. M. or P. C. M., C. G. M. or P. C. G. M., has the authority to install the officers.

PUBLIC INSTALLATION.

The Knights assemble in their hall. The Temple is opened in the Third Degree. The necessary preparation is made and instruction given. After which the C. D. M. forms the procession in marching order, the Knights in full dress and regalia. If a Grand Officer or a Past Grand Officer is present, proper respect must be paid to him or them.

THE MARCH

Will be in the usual form, with the exception that the Temple House is carried in the centre of the procession by four Knights.

The procession is marched three times around the hall, the ranks are opened, and the officers are escorted through to the platform.

The Temple House is placed in front of the Chief Mentor, in the centre of the platform, the officers to the right and left of the C. M.

The Sir Knights, if there is room for them, are in the immediate rear of the officers. If there is not sufficient room on the platform, they are placed in the immediate front of the stage.

LADIES' TABERNACLE.

If the Daughters join in the procession in the hall, they march in the rear of the Sir Knights. The Tribunes' place is in rear of the Daughters.

The officers of the Tabernacle are seated on the platform, to the right and left of the Temple officers. If there is room, the other Daughters are seated immediately in the rear; if not, they are seated in the rear of the Sir Knights in front of the stage. All are seated.

THE CEREMONY.

Music; or, if there is no band, the following hymn is sung:

OUR KING.

I.

The Lord, Jehovah reigns;
  His throne is built on high;
The garments he assumes
  Are light and majesty.
His glories shine with beams so bright,
No mortal eye can bear the sight.

II.

The thunders of His hand
  Keep the wide world in awe;
His wrath and justice stand
  To guard His holy law;
And where His love resolves to bless,
His truth confirms and seals the grace.

III.

Through all His ancient works
  Surprising wisdom shines;
Confounds the powers of hell,
  And breaks their cursed designs.
Strong is His arm, and shall fulfil
His great decrees, His sov'reign will.

IV.

And can this mighty King
  Of Glory condescend?
And will He write His name
  My "Father," and my "Friend?"
I love His name; I love His Word:
Join, all my powers, and praise the Lord.

The Chief Mentor calls up the Knights and Daughters, and the installing officer announces the business that is to be transacted, and states that, so important are the duties that devolve upon the officers that are to be installed, it is of the greatest importance that the guidance and blessing of our King, the Mighty Jehovah, remain with them. Our Chief Orator will now address the Almighty Father, our Sovereign Commander, in prayer.

PRAYER.

O Lord, Thy mercy, our sure hope,
  The highest orb of heaven transcends;
Thy sacred truth's unmeasured scope
  Beyond the spreading sky extends.

Thy justice, like the hills, remains;
  Unfathom'd depths Thy judgments are;
Thy providence the world sustains;
  The whole creation is Thy care.

Since of Thy goodness all partake,
With what assurance should the just
Thy shelt'ring wings their refuge make,
And Knights and Daughters in Thee trust!

Such guests shall be to Thy Temple led,
To banquet on Thy love's repast,
And drink, as from a fountain's head,
Of joys that shall forever last.

How various, Lord, Thy works are found,
For which Thy wisdom we adore!
The earth is with Thy treasure crown'd,
Till nature's hand can grasp no more.

All creatures, both of sea and land,
In sense of common want agree;
All wait on Thy dispensing hand,
And have their daily alms from Thee.

They gather what Thy stores disperse,
Without their trouble to provide;
Thou op'st Thy hand, the universe,
The craving world, is all supplied.

Thou for a moment hid'st Thy face,
The num'rous ranks of creatures mourn;
Thou tak'st their breath, all nature's race
Decay, and to their dust return.

Again, Thou send'st Thy Spirit forth,
Inspiring vital energies;
Nature's restored; replenished earth,
Joyous, her new creation sees.

Thus through successive ages stands
Firm fixed Thy providential care;
Pleased with the work of Thine own hands,
Thou dost the waste of time repair.

Direct us, O Lord, in all our doings, with Thy most gracious favor, and further us with Thy continual help, that in all our works begun, continued, and ended in Thee, we may glorify Thy Holy Name, and finally by Thy mercy obtain everlasting life, through Jesus Christ our Lord, who hath taught us to pray unto Thee, O Almighty Father, in His prevailing name and words. Amen, and amen.

All are seated. Music; or the following hymn is sung:

THE THREE MOUNTAINS.

I.

When on Sinai's top I see
God descend in majesty,
To proclaim His holy law,
All my spirit sinks with awe.
When in ecstacy sublime
Tabor's glorious mount I climb,
In the too transporting light,
Darkness rushes o'er my sight.

II.

When on Calvary I rest,
God in flesh made manifest
Shines in my Redeemer's face,
Full of beauty, truth, and grace;
Here I would forever stay,
Weep and gaze my soul away.
Thou art heaven on earth to me,
Lovely, mournful Calvary.

The Chief Drill-Master, under the instruction of the installing officer, forms all the Sir Knights that are to be installed in line in front of the stage, and says:

Most Faithful Sir: I have the honor to present to you the officers elect of ——— Temple No. —. They are now ready to be installed.

The installing officer will draw his sword, and order the officers elect to draw and lay the sword across their breast, with the point resting on the side of the left shoulder, the left hand on the right breast, and repeat the following

OATH OF OFFICE.

I, T. D., do most solemnly and sincerely promise, upon the word of a Taborian Knight, that I will, to the best of my ability, faithfully discharge and fulfil the duties of the office to which I have been elected. I will support and maintain the Constitution, by-laws, rules, and regulations of this Temple, and the Constitution and by-laws, and regulations and edicts of the Grand Temple of the United States of America.

INSTRUCTIONS.

The installing officer then says:

Sir Knights: Having been elected to the important and responsible duties of the several offices in this Temple, we enter upon the duty of installing you with pleasure, believing that you will attend to the interest of the Temple and conduct the business of your stations with fidelity. You will study to improve the usefulness of our Order, realizing the importance of the trust that is committed to your care by your confiding brethren. A firm reliance on the teachings as you find them laid down in our laws, and the practice of those virtues that are inculcated in our rites, and an implicit confidence in the Lord of Lords, will so direct you in the relation in which you are about to be inducted, that you will reflect honor upon your Temple and credit to yourselves.

THE CHARTER.

The Charter is present, and read by the C. O., and its powers explained by the installing officer. The Sir Knights are seated, and the C. D. M. introduces the C. M. elect to be installed.

The C. D. M. says:

Most Faithful Sir: I take pleasure in presenting to you Sir Knight —— ———, who has been elected to the office of Chief Mentor of ——— Temple No. —. He is prepared for installation. [*His sword, cap, and jewel are laid near the Temple House.*]

The installing officer says:

Sir Knight —— ———, before you are inducted into this important office, you will please answer the following questions relative to the office. If you object to any question, or cannot comply with the request, frankly state your objection, and it will relieve you from the responsibilities of the office, and another must be found to fill the station:

THE TEST.

Do you solemnly promise, upon your obligation as a Knight of Tabor, that you will not open the Temple for business unless the Charter is present, and a constitutional quorum?

I do.

Will you execute the laws, rules, and regulations of the Temple with fidelity?

I will.

Will you support and obey the Constitution, by-laws, rules and regulations, and edicts of the Grand Temple of the United States of America, under whose authority you hold your office?

I will.

Will you endeavor to correct the irregularities, purify the morals, inculcate charity, teach benevolence and true friendship, and promote happiness and harmony in your Temple?

I will.

Will you preserve the ritualistic work unalterable, — the solemn ceremonies and instructions, — and continue them as Chief Mentors have done before you?

I will.

Will you promise not to admit into your Temple a Knight that has not been knighted in a regular Temple, or one that is expelled, or suspended, while under that sentence?

I will.

Do you acknowledge that it is impossible to have intercourse with a Temple that does not work under a Charter from the Grand Temple of the Order of Twelve?

I do.

Do you believe that every Sir Knight has a right to his religious opinion, and that you will promise not to permit any denominational discussion in the Temple?

I do.

Will you support the Constitution, rules, regulations, and ritualistic work of the Ladies' Tabernacle, and aid the Daughters in carrying forward the business of their Tabernacle?

I will.

Will you be careful upon whom you confer the degrees, that our Order may be composed of good and true men?

I will.

Will you bind your successor in office to observe the same test that you have taken?

I will. May the Lord help me.

The installing officer then proceeds as follows:

You will now permit me to cover your head with this cap, and present to you this sword. Its hilt in your hand reminds you that it is only to be drawn in defence of liberty, equality, and innocence.

The badge of your office I now invest you with. It is composed of three perfect numbers. It is an appropriate emblem of our Order. It will continually remind you of the great principles upon which our Order is perpetuated.

I commit to your care the Charter of your Temple.

You will carefully guard it as a sacred power and authority that makes your Temple legal. You will also transmit it to your successor in office. I present to you the Holy Constitutions, the great instructor of the Knights. Open this book in faith, and follow its teachings, without faltering or wavering, and you will exert an influence that will be an honor to yourself and a blessing to the Knighthood.

The Constitutions of the National Grand Temple and Tabernacle are hereby presented to you, with the Constitution, Rules, and Regulations of this Temple. I admonish you to consult them diligently, and cause them to be read in your Temple frequently, that all Sir Knights may be informed of their duty.

I now seat you in the official chair. May the Lord, our King, protect and keep you in the strict performance of your official duty.

THE SALUTE AND WELCOME.

The installing officer then says:

Sir Knights, I present to you your Chief.

[*The Knights rise, and present swords; salute, and return swords.*]

Let us welcome our chief.

[*The Knights and Daughters give the honors, and repeat the words* "We welcome," *three times, and give the clap seven times, with the words* "Be faithful."]

The C. D. M. presents the other officers in regular order, by saying:

Most Faithful Sir: I present Sir Knight —— ———, who has been elected to the office of Vice-Mentor, and is now ready to be installed.

VICE-MENTOR.

Sir Knight —— ———, you have been elected to the office of Vice-Mentor of ——— Temple, No. —, and now invested with the badge of your office. Your duty is to fulfil the duties of the Chief Mentor when that officer is absent; and in his presence you are to counsel and aid him in the government of the Temple. You will now be seated, and may you faithfully perform your duty.

CHIEF SCRIBE.

Sir Knight —— ———, you have been honored by the suffrage of your brethren to the very responsible office of Chief Scribe. I take pleasure in presenting you the badge of your office.

The Chief Scribe shall keep the books of the Temple, — the records and the roll of members. You shall keep a regular account with each member, and collect all dues, fines, and other moneys belonging to the Temple, and pay them into the treasury. You shall record the doings of each meeting plainly and neatly, and report to the Temple, when called on, the condition of the treasury. You shall make a regular report of the Temple, at the regular meeting in the month of July. You shall draw all orders for money on the treasury, and see that they are signed by the C. M., and countersigned by yourself. It will be your duty to make an annual report to the Grand Temple, with list of all the members. You are also required to make a monthly report to the Grand Chief of the condition of your Temple.

You will now be seated. Be thou faithful to duty.

ASSISTANT SCRIBE.

Sir Knight —— ———, you have been elected Assistant Scribe, and I now invest you with the badge of your office.

It shall be your duty to assist the Chief Scribe in the several duties of his office, and in the absence of that officer you are to fulfil all his duties. You will be seated. May you honorably fulfil the duties of your station.

CHIEF TREASURER.

Sir Knight —— ———, by the will of your brethren, you are called to the station of Treasurer of this Temple, and I now invest you with the badge of your office.

The Chief Treasurer shall receive all the moneys and valuables belonging to the Temple, and pay all orders when drawn properly. You shall keep a correct account of all moneys received and paid out. You shall report, when called on by the C. M., the condition of the treasury. You shall make a regular report at the regular meeting in July. You shall give a bond to secure the money of the Temple, to the C. M., C. O., and C. S., for the faithful application of the Temple's money, per Constitution, — the amount of the bond to be agreed on at a regular meeting of the Temple. You shall give to your successor a written statement of the condition of the treasury. You shall, when your successor is qualified, turn over to him all books, cash, papers, and other property that is in your possession.

You will now be seated. Let integrity, probity, and faithfulness guide you.

CHIEF ORATOR.

Sir Knight —— ———, you have been elected to the high position of Chief Orator of this Temple, and I now invest you with the badge of your office.

It is your duty to conduct the devotional exercises of the Temple, to visit the sick or disabled Knights and Daughters, and to attend to the funeral ceremonies. That you may be thoroughly qualified for the work, I present you this Holy Volume. Open and read; it will give you counsel and instruction.

You will now be seated. Be faithful.

CHIEF DRILL-MASTER.

Sir Knight —— ———, it is with pleasure that I find the brethren have honored you by electing you to the station of Chief Drill-Master. I now invest you with the badge of your office and your implement (sword) of duty.

It is your business to instruct the members in the march and drill, and the Taborian sword and javelin exercise. Your station is at the inner door, which I admonish you to guard well during the time of business.

You will now be seated, and look well to your duty.

CHIEF STANDARD-BEARER.

Sir Knight —— ———, I am glad to know that the suffrage of your brethren has placed you in the honorable position of Chief Standard-Bearer of this Temple. I now invest you with the badge of your office.

I also present you the Standard. It is the Banner of our Order. You will carefully keep it, and defend it in the time of danger. It is your duty to carry it on all public occasions, and in all processions.

You will now be seated. Guard well the Banner.

CHIEF GUARDS.

Sir Knights, you have been elected to the office of Chief Guards, and the responsibility of the position requires your constant attendance at the meetings. I now invest you with the badge of your office.

It is your duty to assist the Chief Mentor in giving the several degrees, and to preserve order during the session of the Temple.

You will now be seated. Be faithful to every duty.

CHIEF SENTINEL.

Sir Knight —— ———, you have been elected to attend to the responsible duties of Chief Sentinel, and I now invest you with the badge of office.

I also present to you this sword, and admonish you to use it in defending the post of duty. It shall be the duty of the Chief Sentinel to guard the outside door of the Temple, under the order of the C. M. You shall prepare and keep the Temple in proper order for the meetings. You shall receive such compensation as may be awarded by the Temple for your services.

You will now be seated. Look well to your post.

BOARD OF ATTENDANTS.

Sir Knights, you have been appointed a Board of Attendants. It shall be the duty of the Board to have the oversight of all the members of the Temple, and report to the C. M. when a member is sick or disabled, and what attendance the member needs. Your Board shall draw and pay the sick dues; you shall notify, by order of the C. M., members who are detailed to sit up with sick or disabled members. Your Board shall arrange and prepare the funeral of a deceased Knight. Your Board shall have the oversight of Sir Knights' widows and orphans, and report their condition to the Temple at every regular meeting. Your Board shall keep a book and record its doings, and it shall be your duty to report to the Temple, at the regular monthly meeting, what you have done during the month.

You will now be seated. Be true to duty.

BOARD OF JUDGES.

Sir Knights, you have been appointed a Board of Judges. This is truly an important position, and one of great responsibility, and requires that you should be well acquainted with the laws of our

Order. This Board shall consist of five members, who shall be appointed by the C. M. on the night he is installed. To this Board shall be referred all matters of difference between members, and all trials of members for any offence whatever. This Board shall hold regular meetings, and shall have the power to summon witnesses and the plaintiff and defendant, and carefully hear all sides, make up their decision, and report to the Temple through their secretary. The Temple shall enforce their recommendation, and their action shall be final when approved by the Temple.

You will now be seated. Let justice be your rule and guide.

PROCLAMATION.

The installing officer makes the following proclamation (all the Knights and Daughters standing, except the installed officers):

By the power and authority in us vested, I proclaim that the officers of ——— Temple No. — have been regularly installed, and are now ready for duty for the ensuing term of office. [*The seven claps are given, with the words* "Be Faithful." *All are seated.*]

Music; or the following hymn is sung:

GOLDEN HILL.

I.

Blest be the tie that binds
Our hearts in Christian love;
The fellowship of kindred minds
Is like to that above.

II.

Before our Father's Throne
  We pour our ardent prayers;
Our fears, our hopes, our aims are one, —
  Our comforts and our cares.

III.

We share our mutual woes,
  Our mutual burdens bear;
And often for each other flows
  The sympathizing tear.

IV.

When we asunder part,
  It gives us inward pain;
But we shall still be joined in heart,
  And hope to meet again.

V.

This glorious hope revives
  Our courage by the way;
While each in expectation lives,
  And longs to see the day.

VI.

From sorrow, toil, and pain,
  And sin, we shall be free;
And perfect love and friendship reign
  Through all eternity.

If there is an oration to be delivered, this is the proper time. After which the Knights and Daughters partake of refreshments, and then the Knights assemble, and march and drill. They then march to their hall and close the Temple, and disperse.

BURIAL SERVICE

OF

THE TEMPLE.

BURIAL SERVICE OF THE TEMPLE.

FORM OF PROCESSION.

Chief Sentinel.

Musicians.

Sir Knights.

Chief Color-Bearer.

Two Chief Guards.

Chief Drill-Master.

Vice-Mentor and Chief Orator.

Chief Treasurer.

Past Chief Mentors.

Chief Guard.

Chief Mentor.

Grand and Past Grand Officers.

Officiating Clergy.

* CASKET *
* *
* *

Mourners.

Tabernacles.

BURIAL SERVICE OF THE ORDER OF THE KNIGHTS OF TABOR.

GENERAL INSTRUCTIONS.

1. A Sir Knight, to be buried with the full honors, must be a Key Knight, with the T. D. P., and in good standing in his Temple.

2. When notice of the death of a Sir Knight is received, the Chief Mentor shall summon the Temple to convene, to prepare for the funeral.

3. The Sir Knights must attend in full uniform, with their sword-hilts and banner dressed in mourning, the jewels of the officers in appropriate dress.

4. On the casket of the deceased Sir Knight will be placed his sword and cap (or hat); if an officer, his jewel, clothed in black crape.

5. The day that the body is to be buried, the Knights will assemble in their Temple and march to the residence of the deceased, in the regular order, with swords reversed. The sword and cap of the deceased Knight is borne in the rear of the Chief Mentor. On arriving at the house, the lines open to the right and left. The bearer passes to the casket, and places the sword and cap on it. The pall-bearers (Sir Knights) take the casket, and, led by the Chief Drill-Master, pass down through the lines to the hearse.

6. The procession is then formed, and marched to the church or place of public worship. The Knights will then enter in reversed order, preceding the body, and the mourners follow the body.

7. The Chief Mentor presides during the services, assisted by the Chief Orator. If Grand Officers or Past Grand Officers are present, they must be placed in the procession according to their rank.

8. If the deceased be a Grand or a Past Grand Officer, the Chief Mentor having the jurisdiction will invite the Grand Officers that are present to conduct the burial service.

9. The pall-bearers should be Sir Knights, selected by the Chief Mentor. If the deceased was a member of other secret orders, a portion of the pall-bearers can be taken from them, per agreement, they bearing a part of the funeral expense.

10. While the body is lying in state, there should be two or more Sir Knights on duty near the body, in full dress.

11. The Temple of which the deceased was a member must march nearest the body. If a sojourner, then the Temple having charge of the burial march nearest. Where more than one Temple joins the procession, the youngest takes the lead.

12. When other societies or military unite with the Knights in the burial, they march in front of the Knights.

13. When the head of the procession shall arrive at the place of interment, the lines should be opened, and the Chief Mentor, or the highest officer in rank, preceded by the Chief Drill-Master, pass through, ollowed by the others in order, into the cemetery. On arriving at the grave or vault, they open ranks, and the casket is carried through to the tomb or grave. The coffin is placed over the grave. The Knights form a circle around it, with the family at the foot, and the Chief Mentor, Chief-Orator, and clergy at the head.

14. At the church or place of worship, after the church services over the body, the Temple's services should begin, the Knights standing during the service of prayer.

15. The procession will return to the Temple in the same order that it marched to the grave. A Temple of Knights in procession is positively under the rules of an open Temple; therefore, no Sir Knight can enter or leave the ranks without permission from the Chief Mentor, conveyed through the Chief Drill-Master.

16. Should the Tabernacle join the procession, their carriages or vehicles will follow immediately in the rear of the family. The Daughters wear the same dress as at a Daughter's burial. In the church, their seats are to the left of the Knights. At the grave, they form around the Knights, or at the foot of the grave.

17. When the place of worship or church is not convenient for a part of the services before going to the grave, it may be performed at a more convenient place, or at the grave.

18. The face of the deceased should be uncovered, if possible, during the first part of the ceremony, the Chief Mentor at the head of the casket and the Chief Orator at the foot. The Sir Knights must observe and attend to every command given by the Chief Drill-Master or the Chief Mentor.

THE FUNERAL SERVICE OF SIR KNIGHTS.

After the religious services are concluded, the Sir Knights will commence theirs. Present swords!

FIRST PART.

Chief Mentor. Sir Knights, we are daily reminded of the great lessons of time and eternity. We are mortal. Mortality is written upon all living beings on earth. Man's days are short and fleeting. One by one we pass the gates of death. We are reminded to-day that we are born to die. The great and unfailing truth that death is sure is demonstrated to our view at this sad and mournful hour. The door of our Temple opened to receive a messenger, and there was none to say, "By what right do you enter here?" A brother Knight has been summoned to appear before the Grand Chief of the Universe. His light has been extinguished in the earthly Temple. He lies mute before us. No more will he meet us around the centre square. His voice, so ready in giving knightly greeting, is silent. His hand cannot grasp his sword in defence of innocence, justice, and country. All that remains of our beloved brother Knight is his cold, cold body, stilled in death.

[*The Sir Knights return swords.*]

Sir Knights, let us attend, while the Chief Orator reads to us from the lessons of the Holy Scriptures. May the impressions fill us with meekness and consolation, that we may be prepared when the last of earth comes to us.

Chief Orator. O Lord, remember the faithful among the people, for the children of men fail on earth.

Response. Remember us, O Lord!

C.O. There is not a just man on the earth, that doeth good and sinneth not.

Res. Give ear, O Lord!

C.O. Whatsoever God doeth, it shall be forever; nothing can be put to it, nor any thing taken from it.

Res. Redeem us, O Lord!

C.O. Great are Thy tender mercies, O Lord; quicken us according to Thy judgments.

Res. Redeem us, O Lord!

C.O. We will lift our eyes unto the hills, from whence cometh our help. Our help cometh from the Lord, who made heaven and earth. He that keepeth us will not slumber.

Res. The Lord is my keeper.

C.O. Give thanks unto the Lord, for He is good; because His mercy endureth forever.

Res. Give thanks unto the Lord.

C.O. Lord, make us to know our end, and the measure of our days, that we may know how frail we are. There is but a step between us and death.

Res. Teach us, O Lord!

C.O. God hath made of one blood all nations of men, to dwell on the face of the earth, and hath determined the times before appointed, and the bounds of their habitation.

Res. Be nigh unto us, O Lord!

C.O. The righteous hath hope in his death. Let me die the death of the righteous. Let my last end be like his.

Res. Be merciful unto us, O Lord!

C.O. I know that my Redeemer lives, and that he shall stand at the latter day upon the earth.

Res. May we rest in hope!

C.O. Christ died for us, whether we wake or sleep.

Res. Lord, save us!

[*The Chief Mentor continues:*]

C. M. Will the memory of our brother be forgotten among his brothers?

Res. We will never forget his manly form and virtues.

C. M. Shall his name be recorded in our Temple?

Res. It is recorded here [*hand on heart*]. May he have a clear record in the heavenly Temple.

C. M. He was a true and trusted Knight, and has passed from life's turmoils and struggles. May his soul rest in peace!

Res. May he rest in peace and be happy!

[*The Sir Knights uncover.*]

The following hymn is sung:

"My flesh also shall rest in hope."

I.

Rest for the toiling hand,
  Rest for the anxious brow,
Rest for the weary, way-worn feet,
  Rest from all labor now.

II.

Rest for the fevered brain,
  Rest for the throbbing eye;
Through these parched lips of thine no more
  Shall pass the moan or sigh.

III.

Soon shall the Trump of God
  Give out the welcome sound,
That shakes thy silent chamber-walls,
  And breaks the turf-sealed ground.

IV.

Ye dwellers in the dust,
  Awake! come forth and sing;
Sharp has your frost of winter been,
  But bright shall be your spring.

V.

'T was sown in weakness here;
  'T will then be raised in power;
That which was sown an earthly seed,
  Shall rise a heavenly flower!

The following prayer will then be made by the C. O., or an extemporaneous prayer, if preferred by him; or a clergyman may be invited to pray.

PRAYER.

Holy Lord God, Thou that presidest over the destinies of man, in this hour of sorrow we humbly lift our hearts to Thee. Thou hast mercifully proclaimed in Thy Holy Word that Thou wouldst comfort the mourner, and give consolation to the troubled heart. We worship and adore Thee, Maker of Heaven and Earth, for all things that Thou hast given to us. Cleanse Thou the thoughts of our hearts with the inspiration of Thy Holy Spirit, that we may perfectly love Thee, and worthily magnify Thy adorable name. Be Thou a father to the fatherless, and a husband to the widow, and as God administer consolation to those who are sorrowing this day. We have the evidence before us how frail men are, and how uncertain our continuance on earth is held. We are reminded that our lives are but vapor. Oh, let the light of Thy divine countenance shine upon us, and lead us by Thy grace and Spirit to turn our thoughts to things that make our everlasting peace and happiness. May the burning lamp of Thy pure love light our pathway through the dark valley and shadow of death, that we, by the commendation of Thy beloved Son, our Lord and Saviour, may be enabled to gain admittance to the Heavenly Temple above, and, in the glorious presence of our Lord and Master, enjoy a blissful immortality with the angelic host and the redeemed of earth forever, through Jesus Christ, our Lord. Amen.

Response. Amen, amen, and amen.

The procession will then form, and march to the place of interment in the same order as before.

On arriving at the place, and having formed around the grave, — the casket resting over the grave, — the following hymn is sung:

I.

There is a calm for those who weep,
  A rest for weary pilgrims found;
They softly lie and sweetly sleep,
      Low in the ground.

II.

The storm that racks the wint'ry sky,
  No more disturbs their deep repose
Than summer evening's latest sigh,
      That shuts the rose.

III.

I long to lay this painful head
  And aching heart beneath the soil;
To slumber, in that dreamless bed,
      From all my toil.

IV.

The soul, of origin divine,
  God's glorious image, freed from clay,
In heaven's eternal sphere shall shine,
      A star of day.

V.

The sun is but a spark of fire, —
  A transient meteor in the sky;
The soul, immortal as its Sire,
      Shall never die.

Chief Mentor. Sir Knights, we are assembled to look upon the last of our brother Knight. No more will our voices cheer him in this world of sorrow. No more will he meet us in our pleasant retreat, — the Temple of our love on earth. Our swords cannot now shield him from danger. The Chief Sentinel's challenge will greet his ear no more. He has hailed the entrance for the last time in our Temple. To the silent city of the dead we all must come at last. The manliest form, the bravest heart, that surrounds this spot will be laid captive to death, and bound in the chain of mortality. But he who has been faithful to the teachings of the Chief Mentor of Salvation — the Son of Righteousness — if he can, by the will of the Sovereign Ruler of the Universe, claim a place in the eternal Temple of Bliss, then mortality will only be laid aside to put on the glittering robe of eternal day, and dwell with the royal, happy company in the Temple of Eternal Light.

The sad and solemn assembly here must be forcibly felt by all present. He that now sleeps in death was our brother Knight. With him we have met often around the hollow square; with him we have formed the sacred chain together; we have met life's trials and pleasures. He is now gone beyond our protecting care. That we loved and honored him, our presence here in the dress of our Order tells, and that we revere his memory. We are here to demonstrate our respect for his many good qualities; over his errors and faults, whatever they may have been, to cast the mantle of forgetfulness.

Sir Knights, each successive death-call breaks the chain that binds us to this lower world; makes us pause and reflect what will be our future. If we would meet the Grand Chief of Heaven and Earth in peace and happiness, we must have a clear passport from His hand. Then, when the earthen vessel breaks, our souls will soar away to blissful rest.

The C. D. M. removes the sword and cap from the casket. The Knights present swords. It is lowered into the grave. The C. O. repeats:

C. O. I am the resurrection and the life. He that believeth in Me, though he were dead, yet shall he live. Whosoever liveth and believeth in Me, shall never die. To the earth we commit the mortal remains of our deceased brother. May his soul rest in peace. Earth to earth. [*Cast earth on the casket.*] Dust to dust. [*Cast again.*] Ashes to ashes. [*Cast again.*] Until the morn of the resurrection, when, like our risen Lord and Saviour, may he break every chain and bond of death, and ascend to dwell forever in the sunshine of heavenly beams.

Res. So may it be. Amen, amen.

C. D. M. Sir Knights, return swords.

The V. M. then presents the sword of the deceased to the C. M., who says:

C. M. Sir Knights, you will remember that our deceased brother Knight was taught while in life that this sword, in the hands of a true and trusty

Knight, was an emblem of manly worth ; in his grasp, he was to defend the innocent, protect the weak, have mercy on the fallen, aid the distressed. Be true as steel to a brother Knight. Obey every order given from justice, and silently admonish an erring brother Knight. May the sword of Divine Justice open the way, and permit him to enter the blessed abode of saints and angels, and, in their company and companionship, live forever in the realms of eternal joy.

Res. Amen. So be it. Amen.

The C. T. then presents the key to the C. O., who says :

C. O. This symbol of truth reminds us of Him who said : "I am the way. I am the door. No man can come unto the Father but through Me. I have the keys of death, and the kingdom of heaven." We place this upon the breast of our brother, there to remain as an evidence that he believed in the Divine Being that has power to save to the uttermost. May this hope of our brother in life safely convey his immortal soul, and admit it to the heavenly mansions, to rest forevermore.

Res. Bless the Father. Honor the Son.

The C. O. casts the key into the grave. The Knights uncover, and the C. O. repeats the following prayer :

Our Father which art in heaven, hallowed be Thy name. Thy kingdom come. Thy will be done in earth as it is in heaven. Give us this day our daily bread; and forgive us our trespasses, as we forgive those who trespass against us. And lead us not into temptation, but deliver us from evil. For Thine is the kingdom, and the power, and the glory, for ever. Amen.

Res. Amen, amen, and amen.

The Knights cover, and give the farewell salute three times. Then they form the wall of steel, and sing the following hymn, or some other:

I.

Friend after friend departs:
  Who hath not lost a friend?
There is no union here of hearts
  That finds not here an end;
Were this frail world our final rest,
Living or dying, none were blest.

II.

Beyond the flight of time,
  Beyond this vale of death,
There surely is some blessed clime
  Where life is not a breath,—
Nor life's affections transient fire,
Whose sparks fly upward to expire.

III.

There is a world above,
  Where parting is unknown,—
A whole eternity of love,
  Formed for the good alone;
And faith beholds the dying here
Translated to that happier sphere.

IV.

Thus star by star declines,
  Till all are passed away,
As morning high and higher shines,
  To pure and perfect day;
Nor sink those stars in empty night, —
They hide themselves in heaven's own light.

The C. O. gives the benediction, the lines are formed, and they march back to their hall; and after the business is finished, the Temple is closed.

GRAND TABERNACLE JEWELS.

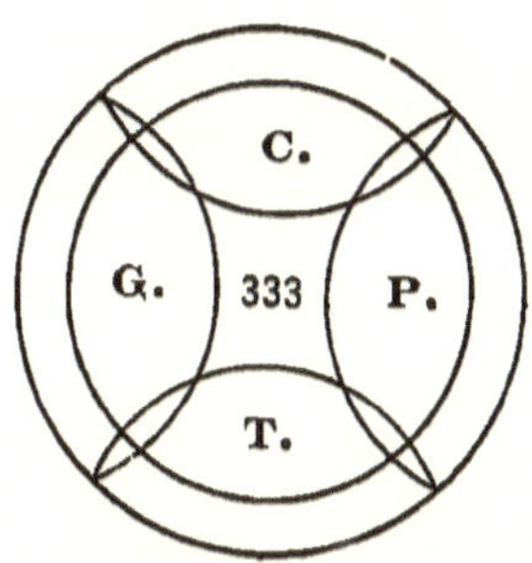

TABERNACLE JEWELS.

(Made of Silver.)

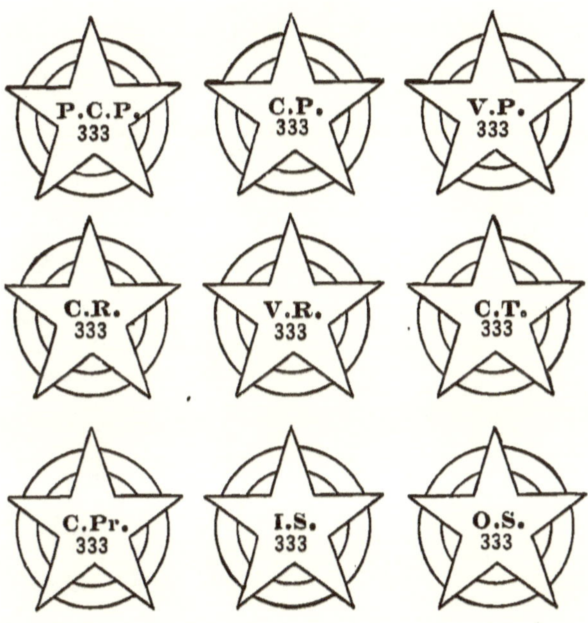

CONSTITUTION

OF THE

LADIES' TABERNACLE.

CONSTITUTION

OF THE

LADIES' TABERNACLE.

ARTICLE I.

SECTION 1. This Tabernacle shall be known by name as ——— No. —, of ———, State of ———.

OFFICERS.

1. Chief Preceptress, ... C. P.
2. Vice-Preceptress, ... V. P.
3. Chief Recorder, ... C. R.
4. Vice-Recorder, ... V. R.
5. Chief Treasurer, ... C. T.
6. Chief Priestess, ... C. Pr.
7. Inner Sentinel, ... I. S.
8. Outer Sentinel, ... O. S.
9. Chief Tribune, ... C. T.
10. Chief Tribune, ... C. T.
11. Chief Tribune, ... C. T.

BOARD OF VISITORS.	BOARD OF EXAMINERS.
1 . . . . B. V.	1 . . . . B. E.
2 . . . . B. V.	2 . . . . B. E.
3 . . . . B. V.	3 . . . . B. E.

Sec. 2. The officers shall be elected at the regular meeting in the month of April, and installed on or before the last Wednesday in the month of May of each year.

Sec. 3. A majority of all votes cast will be necessary to elect; the Tribunes to act as tellers, and announce the vote and result.

Sec. 4. The Board of Visitors and the Board of Examiners shall be appointed by the Chief Preceptress at the regular meeting in the month of May, or at the installation.

Sec. 5. To make the business of the Tabernacle legal, the warrant must be in the hall or room where the Tabernacle opens. The Chief Preceptress or Vice-Preceptress must be present, or the Tabernacle cannot open. Should it happen that the above officers are sick, or disabled, or out of the city, or disqualified, and cannot be present, the members must apply by petition to the Chief Grand Mentor for a dispensation to open the Tabernacle.

Sec. 6. Seven members shall constitute a quorum for any business of the Tabernacle. No meetings can be held nor any business be legally transacted unless a quorum be present, or a dispensation be granted by the Grand Chief.

ARTICLE II.

DUTIES OF OFFICERS.

Sec. 1. It shall be the duty of the C. P. to

preside at all meetings of the Tabernacle, call special meetings when business requires them, decide all questions of order or rules, sign all money-orders, preserve order, enforce the laws, instruct the candidates in the several degrees, and cause the members to learn well the Ritual.

VICE-PRECEPTRESS.

SEC. 2. The V. P. shall fill the duties of the C. P. when the Chief Preceptress is absent.

CHIEF RECORDER.

SEC. 3. It shall be the duty of the C. R. to keep the proceedings of each meeting and the business, under proper heads. She shall have the minute, the roll, and account-books in her possession. She shall issue all notices, draw all drafts on the Treasurer, receive and record all money received into the Tabernacle, pay all money she receives into the Treasury, make an annual report in full to the Grand Temple, and report every three months the condition of the Tabernacle to the members and the Grand Chief. She shall notify the C. G. S. within five days after the expulsion of a member, and for what they were expelled; fill out, and sign and seal all certificates by order of the Tabernacle.

VICE-RECORDER.

SEC. 4. It shall be the duty of the V. R. to assist the C. R. in her several duties, and attend to all the business of the office in the absence of the C. R. It shall be the V. R.'s duty to correspond with other Tabernacles, and conduct the correspondence of the Tabernacle.

CHIEF TREASURER.

SEC. 5. It shall be the duty of the C. T. to receive the funds coming into the Tabernacle from the C. R., keep an accurate account, and pay all drafts. She shall report the condition of the Treasury every three months to the Tabernacle. All money coming into the Treasury, except a certain amount fixed by the Tabernacle, shall be banked in the name of the Tabernacle, and the bank-book kept by the C. T. No money can be drawn from the Treasury but by order signed by the C. P. and countersigned by the C. R., with the seal of the Tabernacle, every order dated and numbered. The C. T. shall give a bond to the Trustees for any amount agreed on by the Tabernacle, with two sufficient securities, for the application of the Tabernacle money under the order of the Tabernacle, before entering upon duty as C. T. She shall hold her office until her successor is qualified.

CHIEF PRIESTESS.

SEC. 6. The C. Pr. shall be present at every meeting, and open it with devotional exercises, give counsel to the sick or disabled members, and instruct candidates on the sacredness of their obligation.

INNER AND OUTER CENTINELS.

SEC. 7. It shall be the duty of the I. S. and O. S. to guard the entrance to the Tabernacle, and perform such other duties as are found in the Ritual.

TRIBUNES.

SEC. 8. It shall be the duty of the Tribunes to assist the C. P. in conferring the degrees, and arrange the hall for meeting, conduct all public business, and attend every meeting. They shall be members of the Tabernacle during their term of office.

BOARD OF VISITORS.

SEC. 9. This Board shall consist of three members, whose duty it shall be to visit the members in regular order, and report any that are so sick or disabled that they need aid and attendance. Their business is to attend, and report to the C. P. the condition of the members. They shall cause orders to be drawn on the Treasury for all weekly benefits, and pay it to the member. They shall report their business to every regular meeting, in a regular written report, signed by all the Board.

BOARD OF EXAMINERS.

SEC. 10. This Board shall consist of three members, whose duty it shall be to examine any matter or business of the Tabernacle that is referred to them. They shall prepare candidates for the degrees, and shall conduct visitors to proper seats. They shall make a regular written report to every regular meeting, signed by all the Board.

BOARD OF TRUSTEES.

SEC. 11. The Board of Trustees shall be the following officers of the Tabernacle: The Chief Preceptress, Chief Recorder, and Chief Priestess. During their term of office, it shall be their duty to look after the material interests of the Tabernacle, and audit the books and accounts of the C. R. and C. T. annually, and report at the stated meeting in April.

ARTICLE III.

MEMBERSHIP.

SECTION 1. The Tabernacle shall not initiate into the mysteries of the Order any woman who is not a lady in actions, manners, and disposition, sound mind, healthy, free from bodily infirmities, a firm believer in the Supreme Being, and aged not less than sixteen years.

SEC. 2. All applications for membership shall be by petition, with name and residence, inclosing fees ———, with the name of a member as the recommender. The petition shall be read at the stated meeting, and if the petitioner is well known to the members, the ballot can be had immediately; if the petitioner is not well known to the members, the petition must be referred to the Board of Examiners, to be reported on at the next stated meeting, and on their report a ballot must be had.

BALLOTING ON PETITION.

SEC. 3. Every application for membership shall be balloted for separately, at a stated meeting. The ballot-box shall be placed on the Tabernacle House, the C. R. calling the roll, and the members voting as their names are called. The ballots shall be white and black. Should four or more black balls appear in the box, the applicant shall be declared by the C. P. rejected. If there is any doubt, and for fear that a mistake has been made, the vote can be had over. The C. P. examines the ballots and announces the election or rejection.

ELECTION TO MEMBERSHIP.

SEC. 4. When an applicant has been elected, and fails to present herself for initiation or admission within three months after being notified (unless prevented by unavoidable reasons), she shall forfeit the amount that has been paid to the Tabernacle. When an applicant has been rejected, her money shall be returned to her, and she is permitted to petition again at the expiration of three months, to the same Tabernacle, or any other in the same city, or wherever the applicant resides.

ARTICLE IV.

THE DEGREES.

SECTION 1. The degrees of the Tabernacle shall be known and styled: (1) Adoption; (2) Advance; (3) The Sealed Daughter. The degrees can be conferred at one meeting, but it is best for the candidate that they be conferred at separate meetings, one degree at a time. The degrees must be given at a meeting called for that purpose.

SEC. 2. No degree shall be conferred until the fee has been paid to the C. R. The fees shall be named in the by-laws of the Tabernacle.

ARTICLE V.

MEMBERS.

SECTION 1. Every member shall pay into the treasury, as monthly dues, the sum fixed in the by-laws, the dues to commence at the first stated meeting after receiving Adoption.

BENEFITS.

SEC. 2. Every member who has passed the probation fixed by the by-laws, and has received the Sealed Daughter, shall be entitled to weekly benefits, and other benefits prescribed in this Constitution.

ARTICLE VI.

DUTIES OF MEMBERS.

SECTION 1. It shall be the duty of every member

to be present at and assist in the business of every regular or called meeting of the Tabernacle.

SEC. 2. The members shall attend, in regular order, to the comforts and needs of sick or disabled members, when notified by the presiding officer.

SEC. 3. Members must cultivate true friendship for each other, and live in love and harmony together, and defend and protect the good name of every true Daughter.

SEC. 4. That the business and expense of the Tabernacle may be kept in a healthy condition, and be a benefit to all of its members, it is the imperative duty of every member to pay her dues and assessments punctually and regularly.

SEC. 5. It is the duty of a member who is about to take a journey, and be gone from home for a short or long time, to take a certificate, as an evidence to other Tabernacles that she, the bearer, is in good standing.

SEC. 6. It is the duty of home members to make the visits of members of sister Tabernacles pleasant and agreeable. Remember that all Daughters are included in the Grand Chain.

SEC. 7. Aid and support the officers in their several duties; be a prop and stay to them, that the Tabernacle may maintain a good name in the community. Finally, let every member, officers and all, try their very best to make our Tabernacle the most pleasant place to meet in on earth, and the Daughters a pattern of social friendship.

ARTICLE VII.

BENEFITS AND RIGHTS.

SECTION 1. Every member shall be entitled to the following benefits and rights:

1. She shall have the right to visit and meet in her own or any other Tabernacle.

2. She shall have the right to turn out with her own or any other Tabernacle in public procession.

3. She shall have the right to take part in any business of the Tabernacle of which she may be a member.

4. It is her right to receive, when sick or disabled so as to need the attention of a physician, the regular weekly benefits, and attendance of the Daughters.

5. It is her right, when poor and needy, or in distress, to receive aid and comfort from every Daughter or Sir Knight.

6. It is her right to travel with a certificate from her Tabernacle, and be received into any other Tabernacle.

7. It is her right to receive an honorable interment by the members of the Tabernacle, and when she has breathed her last on earth, loving hands will prepare her remains for burial.

8. The above rights and benefits are only given to Sealed Daughters.

9. And when they do not receive them from the Tabernacle, it is evident that they are not in good standing, and have forfeited their rights by some action contrary to rule and law.

ARTICLE VIII.

A FORFEITURE OF BENEFITS AND RIGHTS.

Section 1. When members permit their dues to remain unpaid for three consecutive months, the C. R. shall announce the name of the member at any regular meeting, stating that the member is three months in arrears. If said member fails to pay within thirty days after the announcement, she forfeits her rights to all the benefits of the Tabernacle until all dues and assessments are paid.

Sec. 2. A member who is suspended, for a definite or an indefinite time, forfeits her right to all the benefits of the Tabernacle until she is restored.

Sec. 3. A member who is expelled is dead to every right and privilege, and forfeits her right to all the benefits of the Tabernacle until she is restored by an action of the Tabernacle, at a special meeting, and a notice of the restoration given to the Chief Grand Scribe.

ARTICLE IX.

THE GRAND TEMPLE.

Section 1. The Chief Preceptress and Tribunes are the representatives of the Tabernacle in the Grand Temple; one can act for all, if all are not present.

Sec. 2. A Tabernacle has three votes in the Grand Temple, the votes to be cast by their Chief Preceptress, Tribunes, or proxies.

TABERNACLE.

Sec. 3. The Tabernacle must bear the expenses of their delegates to and from the annual or called sessions of the Grand Temple.

Sec. 4. The C. R. sends to the annual Grand Session a full list of the names of the officers and members, with the name and number of the Tabernacle, and the amount of money due to the Grand Temple; also, the number that have been received during the year, the names of those that have died, been suspended, or expelled during the year.

Sec. 5. The Tabernacle shall pay into the treasury of the Grand Temple ——— annually for each member.

Sec. 6. A Tabernacle that fails to report to the Grand Temple for two consecutive years shall be visited by the Grand Chief, or his deputy; and if he finds it is only neglect on the part of the members, he shall arrest their warrant, and report to the Grand Session.

ARTICLE X.

OF TABERNACLES.

Section 1. The Tabernacle is intimately connected with the Temple, and under the same general government; therefore, it is best that they meet in the same hall or rooms.

Sec. 2. Tabernacles must have, within one year after they are warranted, all their furniture and paraphernalia needed to do the work and business.

Sec. 3. The furniture is a Tabernacle House, stations, and tables for the C. R., C. T., and C. P.; rods for the I. S. and O. S.; a crook for the C. Pr., and a chair for each member; pins in the reception room for the working regalia, and closets in the preparation-room. The Tabernacle House shall be furnished with five candlesticks, two cups, a pair of golden shoes, a small Bible, a ball of wool, a roll of flax, a girdle made of white, purple, and scarlet; a pink robe to represent valor; a white robe to represent truth, and a blue robe to represent honor.

ARTICLE XI.

Section 1. The dress of the Daughters shall be brown, trimmed with white; or white, trimmed with gold or yellow, made of any material agreed on by the Tabernacle. All must be alike in material and make.

Sec. 2. The regalia shall be, a light pink collar, trimmed with gold fringe and lace, twelve silver stars, and a pink sash around the waist, trimmed with gold fringe and lace; the regalia to be made of silk, velvet, satin, delaine, or alpaca.

Sec. 3. The head-dress, a golden coronet, white gloves, with gauntlets.

Sec. 4. The regalia of the Chief Preceptress shall be pea-green, trimmed with gold fringe and lace, and silver stars; the sash the same color; pink gloves and gauntlets, a staff four feet long and one inch in diameter, color pink, with a golden ball.

Sec. 5. Members must have their full regalia within ninety days after they are Sealed Daughters.

ARTICLE XII.

PENALTIES AND TRIALS.

Section 1. Every member of the Tabernacle shall be in good standing who is not under charges, or suspended from the privileges and benefits.

Sec. 2. Every member neglecting to pay, and in arrears, and failing to comply with article VIII., section 1, shall be suspended without further action, and remain suspended until all dues and assessments are paid. When the C. R. reports that they have paid up, they shall be reinstated without further action of the Tabernacle.

SEC. 3. Disputes, grievances, and difficulties between members of the Tabernacle can be specified in writing to the C. P., who shall refer the matter to a committee of five Discreet Daughters; this committee shall call the parties before them, examine proofs and witnesses, and report their decision to the C. P. Should the members remain dissatisfied, the C. P. shall lay the whole matter before a called meeting of the Tabernacle, and it shall be decided by a two-thirds vote of all the members present. Should a member prove false, malicious, or a disturber of the peace and harmony of the members, they or she shall be suspended for a definite time, and fined.

SEC. 4. Any member who fails to attend the regular meetings of the Tabernacle for three consecutive meetings, and is without a legal excuse (the only excuse is, out of the city or sick), shall be fined as per by-laws. If she neglects to pay her fine within thirty days, she shall be suspended until it is paid. Seats of officers that are absent for three consecutive meetings, unless excused by a vote of the Tabernacle, shall be declared vacant.

SEC. 5. Every member violating her obligation, the laws, rules, or the regulations of the Constitution or By-Laws, or disclosing the secrets or doings of the Tabernacle, or is found guilty of immoral or criminal conduct, or using improper language, or refusing to come to order when requested by the presiding officer, shall be fined, suspended, or expelled, as may be determined by the Tabernacle, by a two-thirds vote of the members present.

Sec. 6. Any member found guilty of any crime in a criminal court, and who has been sentenced, shall stand expelled as soon as positive proofs are had of the action of the court, and the expulsion shall continue for life.

Sec. 7. Any member who has been suspended or expelled can make an appeal to the Grand Temple. In every instance, the appeal must be given to the C. R. within ten days after the suspension or expulsion. The appeal must be in writing. The appeal must be read in the Tabernacle, and an answer prepared by the Tabernacle, both documents to be forwarded to the C. G. S.

ARTICLE XIII.

PUBLIC PROCESSIONS.

Section. 1. There can be but one public turnout during the year (without a dispensation from the C. G. M.), and that must be in the month of May. This does not include funeral processions for the purpose of burying a deceased member, or for the purpose of receiving a National Grand Officer.

ARTICLE XIV.

OFFICIAL SEAL.

Section 1. The Tabernacle shall have a seal, with the name, number, city, and state, with suitable devices, which shall be affixed to all the official papers of the Tabernacle, an impression of which shall be filed in the office of the C. G. S.

ARTICLE XV.

FEES AND DUES.

Section 1. The fees for the three degrees shall be regulated by the Tabernacle, and published in the by-laws.

Sec. 2. The monthly dues shall not be less than twenty-five cents per month.

Sec. 3. The burial-tax shall not be less than one dollar.

ARTICLE XVI.

BUSINESS.

Section 1. The C. P., when the Treasurer is not able to meet and pay all demands, shall have the power to assess the members, *pro rata*, to make up the deficiency.

Sec. 2. All stated or business meetings must be held in the Third Degree, and members not in possession of that degree cannot be present.

Sec. 3. A member who is outside of the jurisdiction of her Tabernacle, and becomes sick or disabled, may receive her benefits and dues by writing to the C. R., and sending the attending physician's certificate, with directions how to send the money, and the name of the nearest Tabernacle, with the name of the C. R. of that Tabernacle.

SEC. 4. Every Tabernacle can and must make its own by-laws, but they must not conflict with the Constitution of the Grand Temple.

ARTICLE XVII.

RULES OF BUSINESS.

SECTION 1. The Tabernacle must conform to these rules strictly, in the letter and spirit:

FOR STATED OR MONTHLY MEETINGS.

1. At the hour fixed by the by-laws, the presiding officer shall call the Tabernacle to order, and open in form in the Third Degree.
2. The minutes of the last stated and called meetings are read, corrected, and adopted.
3. The report of the Visiting Board is read and approved.
4. Petitions for membership are read and referred, or ordered to ballot.
5. Report of the Board of Examiners.
6. Calling the roll, and receiving dues.
7. Reports of special committees.

8. Unfinished business, and balloting for membership on candidates, etc.

9. New business. Under this rule the quarterly report of the C. R. and C. T. is made, and the annual report is made in the month of July.

10. Lecture on the signs, grips, and words.

11. Close in the proper form.

12. The degrees must be given at a called meeting. All charges and complaints shall be heard and tried at a called meeting.

ARTICLE XVIII.

DEATH.

Section 1. On the death of a member who has been sealed, and is not more than three months in arrears for monthly dues, the Tabernacle shall inter her in a respectable manner. The Tribunes shall attend to all the preparations for the funeral.

Sec. 2. At the next regular meeting of the Tabernacle after the burial of a deceased member, the members shall pay into the treasury a burial-tax of one dollar, in addition to their monthly dues.

Sec. 3. The members of the Tabernacle shall attend the funeral of a deceased member, either on foot or in carriages, wearing their brown dress, black veils trimmed with white, and white gloves. The officers wear a pink and white rosette on the left arm, near the wrist. The C. P. carries her staff.

FUNERAL PROCESSION.

SEC. 4. The Tabernacle will meet at their hall, or some place near the residence of the deceased, and form in the order of march.

ARTICLE XIX.

THE CHIEF PRECEPTRESS.

SECTION 1. This office is one of great responsibility in the Tabernacle. The C. P. should govern with equal and pure justice; be an example in punctuality, politeness, kindness, sisterly love, and calmness; and not administer the law arbitrarily, but with firmness and affection; treat every member with due consideration and honor; be courteous to every member or Daughter; look after and see that a sick or disabled Daughter receives the attention that she should have from the members and Tabernacle; manage the affairs of the Tabernacle so that there will always be sufficient funds in the treasury to meet all necessary expenses; counsel with the members for the interest and good of the Tabernacle; do nothing of importance until she is assured that the members will sustain her; remember that the C. P. is accountable to the Grand Temple for the faithful performance of her several duties: use every honorable means to keep peace and harmony in the Tabernacle.

OTHER OFFICERS.

Sec. 2. All the officers in the Tabernacle have their important duties and responsibilities, — a perfect chain; and if one fails in doing her whole duty, it weakens and mars the utility and usefulness of the Tabernacle. Do your duty well, and your Tabernacle will be a model for other orders and societies.

MEMBERS.

Sec. 3. Every member is equally interested in the success and good name of the Tabernacle. A united effort is required on the part of the members, to make the Order a success.

1. Fulfil every duty and obligation that is required of you, earnestly and constantly.

2. Support and sustain the officers in carrying forward the business of the Tabernacle. Remember that each individual member is obligated in the same way, and has the same responsibility.

3. If there should be any bad feelings arise between the members, try your utmost to have it settled before coming to the Tabernacle. Love and harmony will build up, but confusion and wrangling will tear the Tabernacle down.

ARTICLE XX.

MODE OF TRIAL.

Sections 2, 3, and 4, of article XII., entitled "Penalties and Trials," are plain in telling how to deal with them.

In the cases specified in section 5, the complaint must be made in writing, specifying the nature of the charge, and giving the names of two or more witnesses; this is read by the C. R., at a stated meeting, and referred to a committee of five Daughters, by the C. P.; the time is set for the committee to meet and hear the case, and determine the guilt or innocence of the accused; this committee make their report at a called meeting, called for that purpose.

PENALTIES.

A member convicted of violating the rules or by-laws shall, for the first offence, be fined; second offence, suspended for a definite time; third offence, shall be suspended for not less than one year.

A member convicted of disclosing the secrets and doings of the Tabernacle, or using improper language, shall be suspended for not less than three months.

For criminal or immoral conduct, if the proof is clear, and they are convicted, they shall be expelled.

WHAT IT MEANS.

Suspensions definite mean a fixed time. When that time is out, the member is restored without the action of the Tabernacle.

Suspensions indefinite mean that no time is set. The member can be restored by the action of the Tabernacle, at any stated meeting.

Expulsion means that the member is dead to the Tabernacle; and to resurrect a member and place her again in the Tabernacle, living, will require a two-thirds vote of all the members, at a meeting called for that purpose, notice having been given at the last stated meeting.

CHIEF PRECEPTRESS.

Should complaints be made of the C. P., for incompetency to fulfil the duties of the office, or maladministration, or criminal or immoral conduct, the members, by majority, must make complaint to the nearest C. M. He shall call a meeting of the Tabernacle, and examine the complaints (the C. M. presiding). If the charges are proven, and they are of a nature to injure the Tabernacle, the C. M. shall require two-thirds of the members to sign a petition, stating the complaints and specifications, to the C. G. M. The C. G. M., on the receipt of the petition, shall appoint three C. M.'s, or P. C. M.'s, from three different Temples, whose business it is to try the case and report their decision to the C. G. M. If cleared, she continues in office; if convicted, she is suspended from all official duty until the meeting of the Grand Temple, where the case will be disposed of.

CHIEF TRIBUNES.

The C. T.'s are amenable to their Temple, and all complaints must be made in writing to the C. S. of their Temple.

ARTICLE XXI.

RULES OF ORDER.

1. Every member must appear in the hall cleanly dressed, with white gloves, working regalia, and coronet.

2. Members or visitors will not be permitted to remain in the open Tabernacle unless they have their regalia on.

3. The members shall address the officers in the name of their office.

4. A member speaking shall stand in front of the Tabernacle and address the chief officer, confine herself to the question, and avoid personalities and irrelevant language.

5. A member shall not be interrupted while speaking, except to explain.

6. A member shall not speak more than once on

the same subject, until all who wish to speak have been heard, nor more than twice on any question.

7. No member is permitted to speak longer than ten minutes.

8. No motion shall be in order until it is seconded, and stated by the presiding officer. A motion must be made in writing when requested by the C. R.

9. A motion to lay on the table shall be decided without debate.

10. A motion to postpone carries the question over to the next meeting.

11. When a question is laid on the table, it cannot be taken up until the next meeting, and then only by a two-thirds vote.

12. A motion to reconsider can be acted on only at the same session; it must be made by a member who voted in the majority.

13. The first named on all special committees shall be the chairman.

14. In all business meetings they shall proceed by the order of business.

15. Grand Officers visiting the Tabernacle shall be received standing.

16. A C. G. M. or P. G. M. shall be received with the grand honors.

17. A member wishing to retire from the meeting for the evening must come before the Tabernacle and make the request to the C. P.; she an-

nounces the request, and if a majority vote to grant it, it is done.

18. A member wishing to retire for a few minutes, rises from her seat and stands, with the saluting sign; the C. P. observes her, and returns the sign; that is permission granted.

19. A member crossing the hall during the time the Tabernacle is opened must give the saluting sign.

20. The strictest order and decorum must be kept by the members during the hour of the session.

21. Should an officer be absent from a meeting, the C. P. shall fill the seat *pro tem.*

22. Should an officer be disqualified, resign, be suspended, or expelled, the C. P. shall fill the seat *pro tem.*, until the regular election.

THE EMBLEMS.

The emblem is made of silver or gold. Shape, a half-moon, with 333 in the centre; or the pin or ear-rings can be made in any shape, by attaching to them the half-moon and 333, so they can be seen.

FORM OF PETITION.

To the members of . . . . Tabernacle, No. . . Your petitioner, having a good opinion of the Tabernacle, desires to become a member and be made a Daughter. Age, . . Residence, ...

Enclosed fee, $ . . Recommended by . . . .
. . . day of . . . . A. D. 18 . .
Signed . . . .

FORM OF A CERTIFICATE.

To all whom it may concern,—Greeting:

This is to certify that the bearer, ... is a member in full, and is an S. D. of . . . . Tabernacle, No. . . . of . . . . County of . . . . State of . . . . We recommend this Daughter to all Daughters of the Tabernacle. This certificate to remain in full force for six months, and can be renewed by full payment of monthly dues. Signed this the . . . day of . . . . A. D. 18 . .

{ SEAL } . . . . C. P.

Attest: . . . . C. R.

FORM OF A TRANSFER.

This is to certify that the bearer, Daughter . . . . a member in full of . . . . Tabernacle, No. . . . is hereby transferred to . . . . Tabernacle, No. . . This transfer to be presented within thirty days after date. Signed this the . . . day of . . . . A. D. 18 . .

. . . . C. P.

{ SEAL }

. . . . C. R.

FORM OF TABERNACLE HOUSE.

The house shall be three stories high. First story, fifteen inches square, twelve inches high; second story, ten inches square, twelve inches high; third story, open on four columns, fifteen inches high. Color: First story, pink; second story, pea-green; third story, white.

Rings for carrying; two pink poles.

The moulding of the Tabernacle can be gilded and ornamented to suit the taste.

Lettering on first story, first side, the name and number; second side, the date of warrant; third side, "Daughters of the Tabernacle;" fourth side, the name of city and state.

Second story, first side, 333; second side, the Bible; third side, the cups; fourth side, the golden shoes.

RODS.

The rods for the I. S. and O. S. shall be nine feet long and one inch in diameter, pink color, with golden acorn.

The rod for the Chief Priestess shall be white, same length as above, with pink ball and crook.

The Tribunes' spears shall be five feet long and one inch in diameter, and the color green, with spear-head of silver.

The Chief Preceptress's staff shall be four feet long and one inch in diameter, color pink, and golden ball.

The banner, color pink, with letters and devices to suit the Tabernacle.

AMENDMENT.

The Constitution can only be amended by submitting the amendment in writing to the Grand Temple, and by a two-thirds vote of the Grand Temple any alteration or amendment shall become a law.

The amendment or alteration must be submitted by a majority of the Tabernacles.

NOTICE.

For a book of ceremonies, marching, funerals, dedicating, consecrating, drills, etc., get Dickson's Temple and Tabernacle Manual.

DAUGHTERS' EMBLEMS.

(Gold or Silver.)

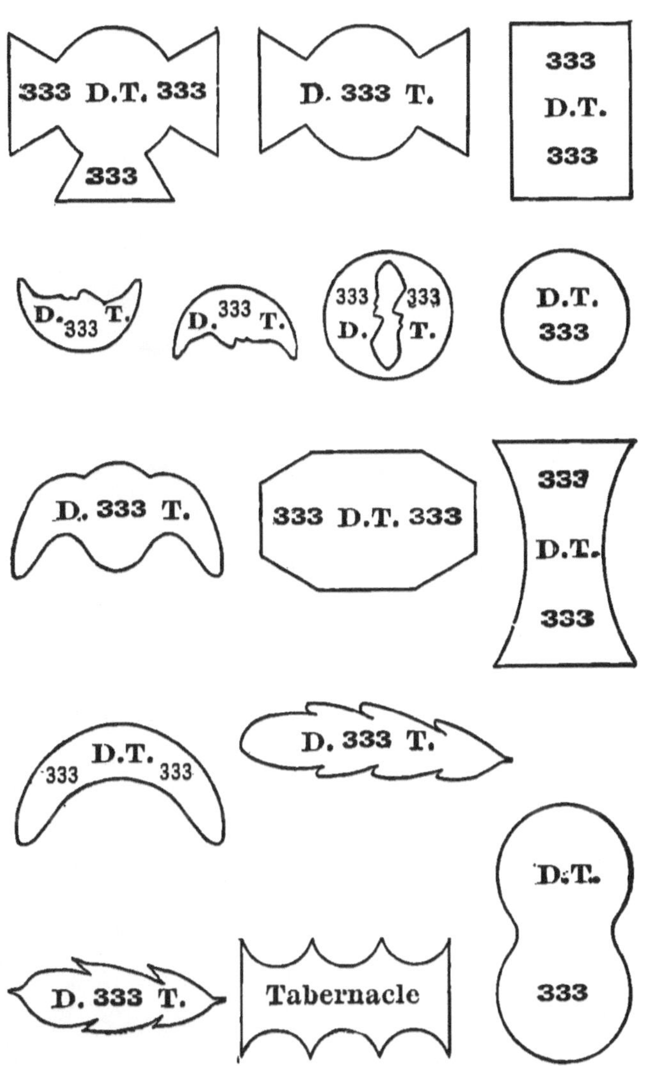

FORM OF TABERNACLE.

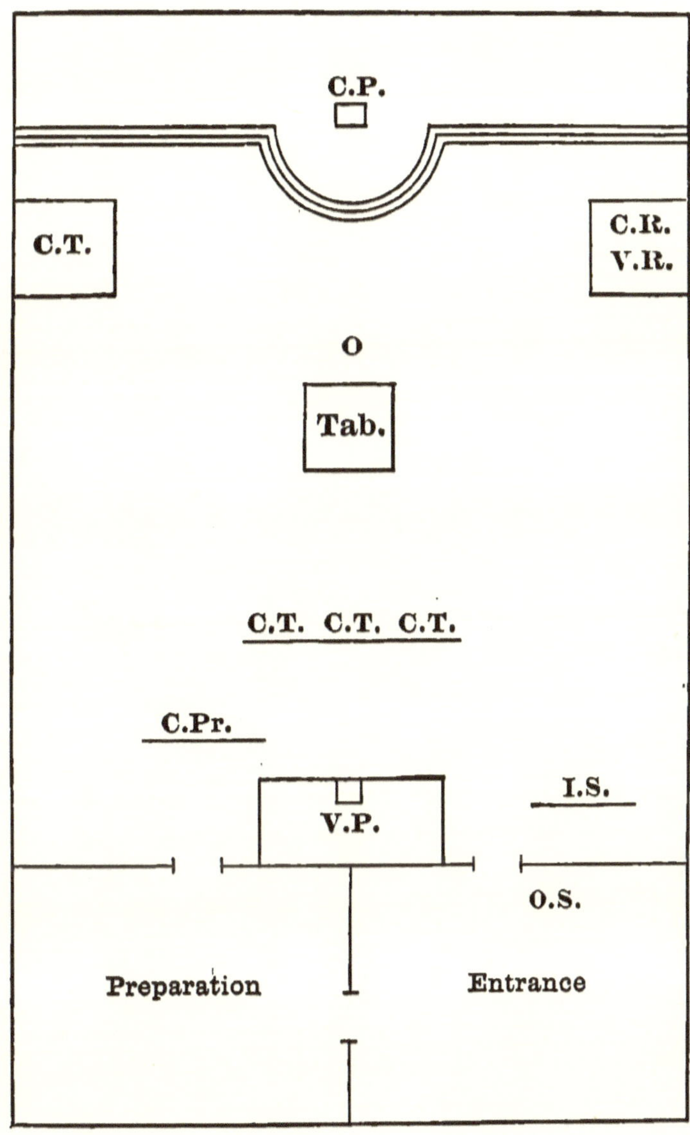

INSTALLATION CEREMONY.

The officers of the Tabernacle can be installed in public or private. The ceremony can be performed by any C. M. or P. C. M., C. G. M. or P. C. G. M.

PUBLIC INSTALLATION.

The Daughters assemble in a room or place near the hall or place where the installation is to be performed, dressed in full regalia, and march in the following order to the place of installation, under the marshalship of one of the Tribunes.

THE PROCESSION.

C. P.
C. T. C. T.
V. P.
C. R. V. R.
C. Pr.
O. S. I. S.
C. T.
B. V. B. V.
B. V.

Marshal.

HOUSE.

B. E. B. E.
B. E., with Banner.
P. C. T. P. C. T.
P. V. P. P. V. P.
Members by Twos.
Sir Knights.

The Tabernacle House is borne by four Daughters. The procession marches three times around the hall. The officers and past officers are seated on the platform, and the members and Sir Knights in front of the platform. The Tabernacle House is placed in front of the Chief Preceptress, in the centre of the platform, the officers to the right and left of her.

THE CEREMONY.

Music; or, if there is no band, the following is sung:

PRAISE TO GOD.

Praise to God, the Great Creator;
  Praise to God from every tongue;
Join, my soul, with every creature,—
  Join the universal song.
Father, source of all compassion,
  Pure, unbounded grace is Thine:
Hail the God of our salvation!
  Praise Him for His love divine.

Joyfully on earth adore Him,
  Till in heaven our song we raise;
Then, enraptured, fall before Him,
  Lost in wonder, love, and praise:
Praise to God, the Great Creator,—
  Father, Son, and Holy Ghost;
Praise Him, every living creature,
  Earth and heaven's united host.

The Chief Preceptress gives three raps, and all the Daughters and Knights stand, while the following prayer is made by the C. O., or some one appointed for that purpose:

Eternal God! Eternal King!
  Ruler of heaven and earth beneath!
From Thee our hopes, our comforts spring;
  In Thee we live, and move, and breathe.
Thy word brought forth the flaming sun,
  The changeful moon, the starry host;
In Thine appointed course they run,
  Till in the final ruin lost.

We lift our hearts to Thee,
  Thou Day-Star from on high!
The sun itself is but Thy shade,
  Yet cheers both earth and sky.
Oh, let Thy rising beams
  Dispel the shades of night;
And let the glories of Thy love
  Come like the morning light!

Turn not Thy face away, O Lord!
  From them that lowly lie,
Lamenting sore their sinful life
  With tears and bitter cry.
Thy mercy-gate stands open wide
  To them that mourn their sin;
Shut not that gate against us, Lord!
  But let us enter in.

Thou knowest, Lord, what things be past,
  And all the things that be;
Thou knowest well what is to come;
  There's nothing hid from Thee.
So press we to Thy mercy-gate,
  Where mercy doth abound,
Imploring pardon for our sin,
  To heal our deadly wound.

O Lord, we need not to repeat
  What we do beg and crave;

For Thou dost know, before we ask,
  The blessing we would have.
Mercy, O Lord! we mercy seek;
  This is the height and sum;
For mercy, Lord, is all our prayer,
  Oh, let Thy mercy come!

And to God the Father, Son,
  And Spirit ever blest,
Eternal Three in One,
  All worship be addressed.
As heretofore, it was, is now,
And shall be so for evermore!
    Amen, amen!

The C. P. gives one rap, and all are seated.

Music; or a hymn is sung, — the following, or any other:

Let all the earth their voices raise,
To sing the choicest psalm of praise;
  To sing and bless Jehovah's name:
His glory let the heathen know,
His wonders to the nations show,
  And all His saving works proclaim.

He framed the globe, He built the sky,
He made the shining worlds on high,
  And reigns complete in glory there:
His beams are majesty and light;
His beauties, how divinely bright!
  His Tabernacle, how divinely fair!

Come the great day, the glorious hour,
When earth shall feel His saving power,
  And barb'rous nations fear His name!
Then shall the race of man confess
The beauty of His holiness,
  And in his Tabernacles His grace proclaim.

The Marshal lights the candles and places them on the Tabernacle House, and places all the officers' jewels on a stand. The officers elect stand in a semicircle. He then says:

Most Faithful Sir —— ——, I have the pleasure of presenting to you the officers elect of ———— Tabernacle, No. ——. They are now ready for installation.

The installing officer then says: You will please open your manuals, and answer the following questions:

Question by the installing officer: Are you willing to serve in the office to which you have been elected?

Answer. I am willing to do the duties pertaining to the office.

Q. Will you punctually attend to the business of your office?

A. I am resolved to attend to all that is required of me under the laws of our Order.

The installing officer then requests them to link their right and left hands together.

They repeat the following words after the officer:

As we are joined together, hand in hand, so we will sustain and support each other in our official duties. We promise to be present at every meeting of the Tabernacle, unless detained at home by sickness, or absent out of the city.

The installing officer gives one rap, and all are seated.

The Marshal then stands the Chief Preceptress elect in front of the Tabernacle House, and says:

Most Faithful Sir, I have the honor of presenting to you Daughter —— ——, who has been elected to preside in this Tabernacle.

The installing officer says:

I thank you, Sir Marshal. You will please give into her hand the Constitution of the Order, and the By-Laws of this Tabernacle.

Installing officer to the Chief Preceptress:

These are the laws of the Order. It is your duty to have them executed promptly; have them read in your Tabernacle at stated times. I now invest you with the emblem of your office, and I present you the staff of power. You will please be seated, and listen. It shall be the duty of the C. P. to preside at all meetings of the Tabernacle, call special meetings, when business requires them, decide all questions of order or rules, sign all money orders, preserve order, enforce the laws, instruct the candidates in the several degrees, and cause the members to learn well the Ritual.

The installing officer gives one rap, and all are seated.

The Marshal says:

I now present —— ———, who was elected Vice-Preceptress of——— Tabernacle, No. —.

The installing officer says:

I now invest you with the emblem of your office. You will please be seated. It is the duty of the Vice-Preceptress to be present at all meetings of the Tabernacle, and assist the Chief Preceptress in her several official duties; and in the absence of the C. P., you are to preside in the meeting of the Tabernacle and attend to the duties of the office.

The Marshal says:

I now present —— ———, who was elected Chief Recorder of ——— Tabernacle, No. —.

The installing officer says:

I now invest you with the emblem of your office. You will please be seated. It shall be the duty of the C. R. to keep the proceedings of each meeting, and the business, under proper heads. You shall have the minute, the roll, and account books in your possession. You shall issue all notices, draw all drafts on the Treasurer, receive and record all moneys received into the Tabernacle, pay all money you receive into the treasury, make an annual report in full to the Grand Temple, and report every three months the condition of the Tabernacle to the members and the Grand Chief. You shall notify the C. G. S., within five days, of the expulsion of a member, and for what she was expelled, and fill out, sign, and seal all certificates by order of the Tabernacle.

The Marshal says:

I now present to you —— ———, who was elected Vice-Recorder of ——— Tabernacle, No. —.

The installing officer says:

I now invest you with the emblem of your office. You will please be seated. It shall be the duty of the V. R. to assist the C. R. in her several duties, and attend to all the business of the office in the absence of the C. R. It shall be the V. R.'s duty to correspond with other Tabernacles, and conduct the correspondence of the Tabernacle.

The Marshal says:

I now present to you —— ———, who was elected Treasurer of ——— Tabernacle, No. —.

The installing officer says:

I now invest you with the emblem of your office. You will please be seated. It shall be the duty of the C. T. to receive the funds coming into the Tabernacle from the C. R., keep an accurate account, and pay all drafts. You shall report the condition of the treasury every three months to the Tabernacle, or at the regular quarterly meeting. Your further duties and instructions you will see in the Constitution.

The Marshal says:

I now present to you —— ———, who was elected Chief Priestess of ——— Tabernacle, No. —.

The installing officer says:

I now invest you with the emblem of your office, and present to you the shepherdess's crook. You will please be seated. The C. Pr. shall be present at every meeting, and open it with devotional exercises, give counsel to the sick or disabled members, and instruct candidates on the sacredness of their obligation. Your office is one of usefulness and benefit. Be true to duty.

The Marshal says:

I now present to you —— —— and —— ——, who were elected Inner and Outer Sentinels of ——— Tabernacle, No. —.

The installing officer says:

I now invest you with the emblems of your offices, and present to you the rods of your authority. You will please be seated. It shall be the duty of the I. S. and O. S. to guard the entrance to the Tabernacle, and perform such other duties as are found in the Ritual. Your punctual and early attendance is absolutely required. Look well to your duty.

The Marshal says:

I now present to you Sir Knights ——— and ———, who have been elected Tribunes of ——— Tabernacle, No. —.

The installing officer says:

I now invest you with the emblems of your offices, and present to you the javelins of authority. You will please be seated. It shall be the duty of the Tribunes to assist the C. P. in conferring the degrees, and arrange the hall for meetings; conduct all public business, and attend every meeting. You will be members of the Tabernacle during your term of office.

The Marshal says:

I now present to you Daughters ———, ———, and ———, who were appointed the Board of Visitors of ——— Tabernacle, No. —.

The installing officer says:

I now invest you with the emblems of your office. You will please be seated. It shall be your duty to visit the members in regular order, and report any who are so sick or disabled that they need aid and attendance. It will also be your duty to attend, and report to the C. P. the condition of the members. You shall cause orders to be drawn on the Treasury for all weekly benefits, and pay them to the members. You shall report your business to every regular meeting, in a written report, signed by all the Board.

The Marshal says:

I now present to you Daughters ———, ———, and ———, who were appointed a Board of Examiners of ——— Tabernacle, No. —.

The installing officer says:

I now present to you the emblem of your office. You will please be seated. It shall be your duty to examine any matter or business of the Tabernacle that is referred to you. You shall prepare candidates for the degrees, and shall conduct visitors to proper seats. You shall make a written report to every regular meeting, signed by all the members of the Board.

The installing officer then gives three raps, and all stand, except the installed officers. He then says:

By the power and authority in us vested, we declare the officers of ——— Tabernacle, No. —, installed and ready for duty for the Tabernacle year ensuing. We declare, we declare!

The Marshal says:

I now proclaim that the officers of ——— Tabernacle, No. —, are installed in regular form.

The Sir Knights and Daughters give five claps,

and say: "We declare." This is given three times. The last time they say: "We declare the officers of ——— Tabernacle, No. —, regularly installed."

The installing officer gives one rap, and all are seated.

Music, or singing; after which, if there is to be an oration, this is the time; and then a march three times around the hall, and then close, — or, if in a public hall, dismiss.

TABERNACLE FURNITURE.

TEMPLE FURNITURE.

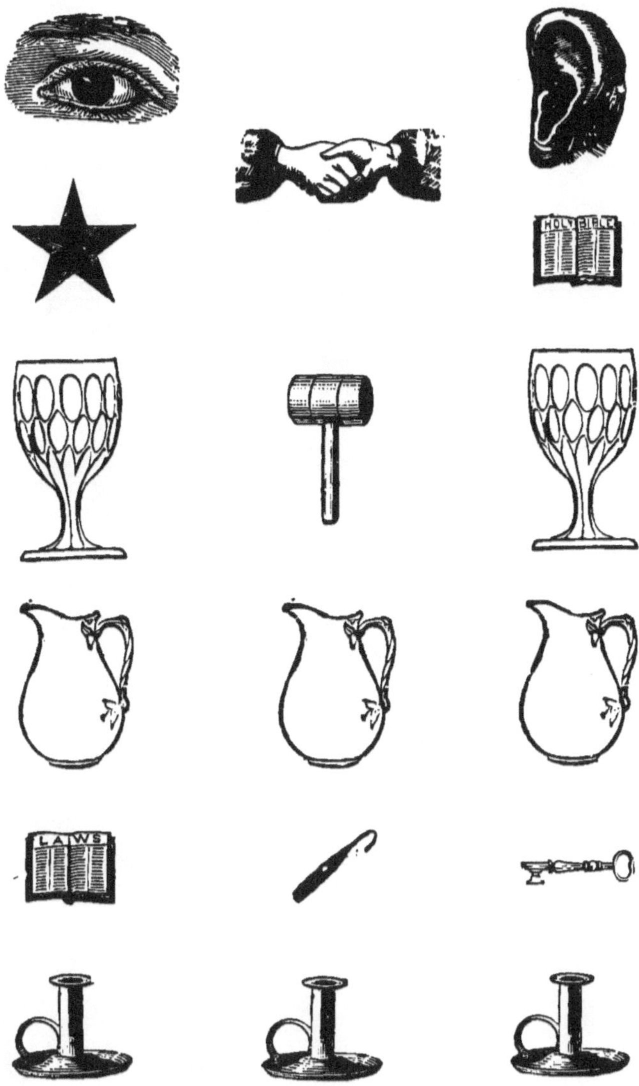

FUNERAL CEREMONIES

OF A

DAUGHTER OF THE TABERNACLE.

FUNERAL CEREMONIES

OF A

DAUGHTER OF THE TABERNACLE.

The ceremonies which are observed at Tabernacle funerals, and for the interment of the dead, are very impressive and appropriate. They are performed as an imperative, yet a sorrowful, duty, and as a token of affection and respect to the memory of a departed Daughter.

DIRECTIONS.

1. No Daughter of the Tabernacle can be buried with the formalities of the Tabernacle unless she is a Sealed Daughter in good standing, and by the consent of her family.

2. The Chief Preceptress, having received notice of the death of a Daughter (the deceased being a Sealed Daughter in good standing), it shall be her duty to issue orders to the Tabernacle to make preparations to attend the funeral, and extend an invitation to the Temples and other Tabernacles. (Should the family of the deceased desire to arrange for the funeral, their wishes must be complied with.)

3. The whole arrangement for a burial of a Daughter by the Tabernacle must be made by the Tribunes. The ceremonies are conducted by the C. O. or C. M. of the nearest Temple.

4. Whenever other societies unite with the Tabernacle in the burial of a Daughter, the body of the deceased must be in charge of the Tabernacle having jurisdiction. Other societies are permitted to perform their ceremonies, but the services of the Tabernacle must not be omitted.

5. If a sojourner, in good standing, dies within the jurisdiction of a Tabernacle, it will be the duty of the Tabernacle to inter her with all the formalities of the Order, or attend to sending the body to its home; where there are two or more Tabernacles, the oldest Tabernacle has precedence, unless otherwise arranged. The Tabernacle of which the deceased sojourner was a member shall pay all expenses incurred in the funeral, to the Tabernacle that attended to this duty.

6. The pall-bearers shall be Sir Knights of Tabor, selected by the Chief Preceptress.

7. No Tabernacle can unite with other societies in the burial of a person not a Daughter or a Knight of Tabor, without a dispensation from the Chief Grand Mentor or the consent of the Grand Temple.

8. The members of the Tabernacle shall attend the funeral of a deceased Daughter, either on foot or in vehicles, wearing brown dresses trimmed with

white, black veils bordered with white, white gloves, and a pink and white rosette on the left shoulder. The officers wear a pink and white rosette on the left arm, near the wrist, and a pink and black rosette on the right shoulder. The C. P. and P. C. P. carry their staffs and a green rosette on the right shoulder. The I. S. and O. S. carry their rods.

9. A Sir Knight attending the funeral of a Daughter shall wear a black suit, white gloves, the regulation collar and cap. The Tribunes shall carry their spears. The C. M.'s and P. C. M.'s wear their swords, trimmed with black. Should a C. G. M. or P. C. G. M. attend, the C. G.'s march in their rear with their swords reversed, the C. S. B., with two assistants, in front of them.

10. When two or more Tabernacles are in procession, the Tabernacle of which the deceased was a member, will march nearest to the corpse. If the deceased member was a member of other secret societies, such society shall bear a part of the funeral expense. In that case, the society that she has been longest a member of can march nearest to the body, and the pall-bearers be equally divided between the societies.

11. A Tabernacle in procession is under the discipline of an open Tabernacle, and no one must leave the ranks without the positive permission of the Chief Preceptress, conveyed through one of the Tribunes, who is acting Marshal.

THE SERVICE.

The Tabernacle will assemble at their hall, or some place, that is proper, near the residence of the deceased. The C. P. will declare the Tabernacle opened, and announce the business that has called them together. The C. R. reads the name and age of the deceased member, how long she has been a member, the day and date of her death, and the date that she was interred. It is enrolled in the record-book.

ORDER OF MARCH.

The procession is formed, and march to the residence of the deceased member, receive the corpse, and march in the following order to the church or place appointed for the services:

Marshal.

Two Tribunes, with spears.
Chief Preceptress.
Past Chief Preceptresses, by twos.
Inner and Outer Sentinels.
Chief and Assistant Recorder.
Vice-Preceptress.
Chief Treasurer and Chief Priestess.
Members, two by two.
Other Tabernacles, in the same order.
Chief Orator and Clergy.

* HEARSE. *
* *
* *

Family.
Knights, in their marching order.
Other Societies.
Carriages.

AT THE CHURCH.

The Tabernacle and Sir Knights will open ranks, and the corpse and family will pass into the church. The Daughters and Knights will follow to seats. After the church ceremony and sermon by a minister or the Chief Orator, the Daughters, Sir Knights, family, and friends will march around and view the body, while the choir chants a funeral anthem, or a hymn is sung by the congregation. The Sir Knights then form in front of the church, and open ranks, when the casket is passed through to the hearse.

MARCH TO THE CEMETERY.

Chief Tribunes.
Chief Orator and Clergy.

* HEARSE. *
* *
* *

Family Carriages.
Daughters in Vehicles.
Other Societies.
Sir Knights.
Other Vehicles.

AT THE GRAVE.

Place the casket over the grave.

The Daughters and Sir Knights form a circle around the grave, with the family at the head, and the C. O. and ministers at the foot. The Daughters and Sir Knights join hands, and sing the following hymn:

Unveil thy bosom, faithful tomb;
Take this now treasure to thy trust,
And give these sacred relics room
To slumber in the silent dust.

Nor pain, nor grief, nor anxious fear,
Invade thy bounds; no mortal woes
Can reach the peaceful sleeper here,
While angels watch the soft repose.

So Jesus slept; God's dying Son
Passed thro' the grave, and blest the bed:
Rest here, blest saint, till from His throne
The morning break, and pierce the shade.

Break from His throne, illustrious morn!
Attend, O earth! His sovereign word:
Restore thy trust; a glorious form
Shall then ascend to meet the Lord!

The Chief Orator — or the minister, if he is a member — then reads the following prayer, the Daughters and Knights holding up their joined hands during the prayer:

O merciful God, the Father of our Lord Jesus Christ, who is the resurrection and the life; in whom whosoever believeth shall live, though he die; and whomsoever liveth and believeth in Him, shall not die eternally; who also hath taught us, by His holy apostle St. Paul, not to be sorry, as men without hope, for those who sleep in Him. We humbly beseech Thee, O Father, to raise us from the death of sin unto the life of righteousness; that when we shall depart this life, we may rest in Him, and that at the general resurrection on the last day, we may be found acceptable in Thy sight, and receive that blessing which Thy well-beloved Son shall then pronounce to all who love and fear Thee, saying: Come, ye blessed children of my Father, receive the kingdom prepared for you from the beginning of the world. Grant this, we beseech Thee, O merciful Father, through Jesus Christ, our Mediator and Redeemer. Amen.

The prayer being ended, all say: "Amen, amen, amen!" raising and lowering their hands slowly, three times.

While the casket is being lowered into the grave, the following hymn is sung:

I.

Dear as thou wert, and justly dear,
We will not weep for thee;
One thought shall check the starting tear,—
It is, that thou art free.

II.

And thus shall faith's consoling power
The tears of love restrain;
Oh, who that saw thy parting hour
Could wish thee back again!

III.

Triumphant in thy closing eye
The hope of glory shone;
Joy breathed in thine expiring sigh,
To think the fight was won.

IV.

Gently the passing spirit fled,
Sustained by grace Divine;
Oh, may such grace on me be shed,
And make my end like thine!

The following exhortation is delivered by the C. O., or the minister, if he is a member:

Daughters, this solemn scene tells us that our Tabernacle has been visited by that dread messenger, Death, against whose certain entrance sentinels and closed doors offer no stay or stop. The chain of our circle has been broken, and a link is gone, never more to return. We mourn the loss of a dear companion. The dead body of our beloved sister, M—— N———, is now before us in its narrow house. This is the last of earthly Tabernacles for her whom we have met so often in our undisturbed retreat, away from the worldly-minded, to enjoy a little season of happiness; and now, we have assembled to bid our sister a last, long farewell. She sleeps with the unnumbered dead. The storms and calms of life have passed over her pathway. She is at rest. Her toils on earth have ended. As it has pleased our Heavenly Father to call the soul of our departed sister from its earthly Tabernacle, may she find joy and happiness in the Tabernacles of that peaceful land where the eternal light and love of the Eternal Father, Son, and Holy Spirit will shed their rays forever, and, in the company of the angelic host and the redeemed of earth, may we meet our loved sister, to part no more.

Farewell, for a little while.

The Chief Orator repeats the following invocation, and the Daughters and Knights respond. At each response they give one clap of the hands:

Chief Orator. Almighty Father, may we realize

that Thine all pervading presence is with us; may Thy spirit perfect us in truth and obedience to Thy will.

Response. May the Lord's will be done.

C.O. May we meet our sister Daughter in the fadeless light of God's kingdom.

Res. Into the Lord's hands we commit our souls.

C.O. Behold, O Lord, we are in sorrow. O Lord, let the light of Thy countenance shine upon us in our distress. Give comfort, and turn our mourning to joy.

Res. The Lord will hear and answer our prayer; only trust Him.

The following hymn is sung:

I.

How still and peaceful is the grave!
  Where, life's vain tumults past,
Th' appointed house, by heaven's decree,
  Receives us all at last.

II.

The wicked there from troubling cease;
  Their passions rage no more;
And there the weary pilgrim rests
  From all the toils he bore.

III.

There rest the prisoners, now released
  From slavery's sad abode:
No more they hear th' oppressor's voice,
  Or dread the tyrant's rod.

IV.

There servants, masters, small and great,
Partake the same repose;
And there, in peace, the ashes mix
Of those who once were foes.

V.

All, levelled by the hand of death,
Lie sleeping in the tomb,
Till God, in judgment, calls them forth,
To meet their final doom.

The ceremonies may conclude with the church order for the burial of the dead, or by the following, read by the C. O.:

Forasmuch as it hath pleased Almighty God, in His wise providence, to take out of this world the soul of our deceased sister, we therefore commit her body to the ground, earth to earth, ashes to ashes, dust to dust; looking for the general resurrection in the last day, and the life of the world to come, through our Lord Jesus Christ; at whose second coming in glorious majesty to judge the world, the earth and the sea shall give up their dead; and the corruptible bodies of those who sleep in Him shall be changed, and made like unto His own glorious body, according to the mighty working whereby He is able to subdue all things unto Himself. Amen.

The services close, and the procession returns to the place from whence they came; and after the necessary business is finished, the Tabernacle is closed.

FORM OF TABERNACLE HOUSE.

DEDICATION CEREMONY.

DEDICATION CEREMONY.

The Temple and Tabernacle can be dedicated either in public or private.

INSTRUCTIONS.

1. The hall, before it is dedicated, must be furnished with all the necessaries for the work and business of the Temple and Tabernacle.

2. The ceremony must be performed by a C.G.M., P. C. G. M., or a D. G. M.

3. The Temple and Tabernacle Houses within the square, with their full furniture in sight, and candles burning.

4. The Daughters are marched into the hall, in full dress and regalia; the officers in their stations, and seated.

5. The Knights, in full dress and regalia, assemble in the anterooms, or some place near the hall, and march into the hall and around three times, and are seated; officers in their stations. Music; or the following hymn is sung:

I.

How lovely are Thy dwellings fair,
Oh, Lord of hosts! How dear
The pleasant Tabernacles are,
Where Thou dost dwell so near.

II.

My soul doth long and, fainting, sigh
  Thy Temples, Lord, to see;
My heart and flesh aloud do cry,
  O, living God, for Thee!

III.

Happy, who in Thy house reside,
  Where Thee they ever praise;
Happy, whose strength in Thee doth bide,
  And in their hearts Thy ways.

IV.

They journey on from strength to strength,
  With joy and gladsome cheer,
Till all before our God, at length,
  In Zion do appear.

The C. M. of the Temple gives three raps, and all stand. He then says:

We have assembled for the purpose of dedicating this hall to the work and business of the Temple and Tabernacle. I now take pleasure in introducing Sir —— ———, the dedicating officer.

The C. M. then presents the gavel to the dedicating officer.

The dedicating officer gives one rap, and all are seated. He then reads as follows:

Sir Knights and Daughters, the solemn duties of the hour, and the importance of the business that has called us together, cannot be overestimated in an Order like ours, fulfilling a high and holy duty in this Christian age. We are banded together for mutual aid and protection; to help each other in sickness; to comfort each other in distress; to support disabled members; to care for the lonely orphans of Knights or Daughters, and make glad the hearts of mourning widows. This is the mission of our beloved Order. Then, how necessary it is that we should, in all our work and business, remember an overruling Providence, and ask that He may preside over our counsels and give us wisdom to successfully conduct and guide the affairs of our Order, that it may continue a blessing for all time to come. Let us not only dedicate our hall to the Lord God, but give ourselves to His keeping.

THE CEREMONY.

The dedicating officer gives three raps, and all stand. He then gives the following commands:

1. Sir Knights, form a hollow square. [The C. M. and C. O. in the centre of the square, near the Temple House.]

2. Sir Knights, Handle Swords!

3. Sir Knights, Draw Swords!

4. Sir Knights, Present Swords!

5. Sir Knights, Deposit Swords. [The swords are laid down, pointing to the Temple and Tabernacle House.]

6. Sir Knights, To the Right About Face! [Turn, face out.] Deposit Caps!

7. Sir Knights, To the Left About Face! [Turn, face in.]

Let us pray.

The Knights will kneel on the right knee, with their arms across their breast, the Daughters standing.

The C. O., standing, will read the following prayer:

O, Eternal God, mighty in power, and of majesty incomprehensible, whom the heaven of heavens cannot contain, much less the walls of Temples made with hands, and who yet hast been graciously pleased to promise Thy especial presence wherever two or three of Thy faithful servants shall assemble in Thy name to offer up their praises and supplications unto Thee; vouchsafe, O Lord, to be present with us, who are here gathered together, with all humility and readiness of heart, to consecrate this place to the honor of Thy great name. Accept, O Lord, this service at our hands, and bless it with such success as may tend most to Thy glory, and the furtherance of our happiness, both temporal and spiritual, through Jesus Christ, our blessed Lord and Saviour. Amen.

All say: Amen, amen, amen.

The C. M. reads as follows:

Blessed be the Lord my strength, which teacheth my hands to war, and my fingers to fight.

My goodness, and my fortress; my high tower and my deliverer; my shield, and He in whom I trust; who subdueth my people under me.

Lord, what is man, that Thou takest knowledge of him! or the son of man, that Thou makest account of him!

Man is like to vanity; his days are as a shadow that passeth away.

Bow Thy heavens, O Lord, and come down; touch the mountains, and they shall smoke.

Cast forth lightning, and scatter them; shoot out Thine arrows, and destroy them.

Send Thine hand from above, rid me, and deliver me out of great waters, from the hand of strange children.

Whose mouth speaketh vanity, and their right hand is a right hand of falsehood.

I will sing a new song unto Thee, O God! upon a psaltery and an instrument of ten strings will I sing praises unto Thee.

It is He that giveth salvation unto kings; who delivereth David his servant from the hurtful sword.

Rid me, and deliver me from the hand of strange children, whose mouth speaketh vanity, and their right hand is a right hand of falsehood.

That our sons may be as plants grown up in their youth; that our daughters may be as corner-stones, polished after the similitude of a palace.

That our garners may be full, affording all manner of store; that our sheep may bring forth thousands and ten thousands in our streets.

That our oxen may be strong to labor; that there be no breaking in, nor going out; that there be no complaining in our streets.

Happy is that people, that is in such a case; yea, happy is that people, whose God is the Lord.

The dedicating officer, standing near the Temple House, says:

Attention, Sir Knights! Stand, and form the living chain.

The Knights arise, and clasp hands all around, so as to form a continuous chain.

The command is then given to the Daughters to form a living chain around the Knights.

The dedicating officer reads from Judges, Chapter IV.:

And the children of Israel again did evil in the sight of the Lord when Ehud was dead.

And the Lord sold them into the hand of Jabin, king of Canaan, that reigned in Hazor, the captain of whose host was Sisera, which dwelt in Harosheth of the Gentiles.

And the children of Israel cried unto the Lord; for he had nine hundred chariots of iron; and twenty years he mightily oppressed the children of Israel.

And Deborah, a prophetess, the wife of Lapidoth, she judged Israel at that time.

And she dwelt under the palm tree of Deborah, between Ramah and Beth-el in Mount Ephraim; and the children of Israel came up to her for judgment.

And she sent and called Barak the son of Abinoam out of Kedesh-naphtali, and said unto him, Hath not the Lord God of Israel commanded, saying, Go, and draw toward Mount Tabor, and take with thee ten thousand men of the children of Naphtali, and of the children of Zebulum?

And I will draw unto thee, to the river Kishon, Sisera, the captain of Jabin's army, with his chariots and his multitude; and I will deliver him into thine hand.

And Barak said unto her, If thou wilt go with me, then I will go; but if thou wilt not go with me, then I will not go.

And she said, I will surely go with thee; notwithstanding the journey that thou takest shall not be for thine honor; for the Lord shall sell Sisera into the hand of a woman. And Deborah arose, and went with Barak to Kedesh.

And Barak called Zebulun and Naphtali to Kedesh; and he went up with ten thousand men at his feet; and Deborah went up with him.

Now Heber, the Kenite, which was of the children of Hobab, the father-in-law of Moses, had severed himself from the Kenites, and pitched his tent unto the plain of Zaanaim, which is by Kedesh.

And they shewed Sisera that Barak, the son of Abinoan, was gone up to Mount Tabor.

And Sisera gathered together all his chariots, even nine hundred chariots of iron, and all the people that were with him, from Harosheth, of the Gentiles, unto the river of Kishon.

And Deborah said unto Barak, Up; for this is the day in which the Lord hath delivered Sisera into thine hand; is not the Lord gone out before thee? So Barak went down from Mount Tabor, and ten thousand men after him.

And the Lord discomfited Sisera, and all his chariots, and all his host, with the edge of the sword before Barak; so that Sisera lighted down off his chariot, and fled away on his feet.

But Barak pursued after the chariots, and after the host, unto Harosheth of the Gentiles; and all the host of Sisera fell upon the edge of the sword; and there was not a man left.

All give three claps, and say, "Well done, well done, well done."

The C. M. says:

Attention, Sir Knights! To the right about face! Recover caps! To the left about face! Recover swords! Present swords! Return swords! Form procession! March around the hall, Daughters in front!

The dedicating officer gives one rap, and all are seated. Music; or the following hymn is sung:

I.

The spacious earth is all the Lord's,
The Lord's her fulness is;
The world, and they that dwell therein,
By sovereign right are His.

II.

He framed and fix'd it on the seas;
And His almighty hand
Upon inconstant floods has made
The stable fabric stand.

III.

But for Himself this Lord of all
One chosen seat design'd;
Oh! who shall to that sacred hill
Deserved admittance find?

IV.

The man whose hands and heart are pure,
  Whose thoughts from pride are free;
Who honest poverty prefers
  To gainful perjury;

V.

This, this is he, on whom the Lord
  Shall shower His blessings down;
Whom God, His Savior, shall vouchsafe
  With righteousness to crown.

The dedicating officer gives three raps, and says:

Sir Knights and Daughters, please form a living circle around the Temple and Tabernacle (the dedicating officer, C. M., and C. P. in the centre).

The dedicating officer gives two raps on the Temple and Tabernacle-Houses, and at the same time pronouncing:

In the name of the Lord God of Heaven, earth, and the universe, in whom is all glory and power, I do solemnly dedicate this hall to the work of the Temple and Tabernacle.

All give one clap, and pronounce, "May He bless the work."

The dedicating officer gives four raps on the Temple and Tabernacle Houses, and says:

In the name of Barak, the son of Abinoam, I do

solemnly dedicate this hall to Charity and Friendship.

All give two claps, and pronounce, "May we hear and obey."

The dedicating officer gives six raps on the Temple and Tabernacle Houses, and says:

In the name of Deborah, the prophetess, I do solemnly dedicate this hall to Honor and Virtue.

All give three claps, and pronounce, "May we remember." All join hands, and the C. O. addresses the Lord of all:

O, Most Glorious Lord, we acknowledge that we are not worthy to offer unto Thee any thing belonging unto us; yet we beseech Thee, in Thy great goodness, graciously to accept the dedication of this place to Thy service, and to prosper this our undertaking. Receive the prayers and intercessions of all those who shall call upon Thee in this house, and give them grace to prepare their hearts to serve Thee with reverence and godly fear; affect them with an awful apprehension of Thy divine majesty, and a deep sense of their own unworthiness; that, so approaching Thy sanctuary with lowliness and devotion, and coming before Thee with clean thoughts and pure hearts, with bodies undefiled, and minds sanctified, they may always perform a service acceptable to Thee, through Jesus Christ our Lord. Amen, amen, amen.

The procession is formed, and they march around the hall three times. Music; or the following hymn is sung:

I.

Ye boundless realms of joy,
  Exalt your Maker's fame;
His praise your song employ
  Above the starry frame:
      Your voices raise,
    Ye Cherubim
    And Seraphim,
      To sing His praise.

II.

Thou moon, that rul'st the night,
  And sun that guid'st the day,
Ye glitt'ring stars of light,
  To Him your homage pay:
      His praise declare,
    Ye heavens above,
    And clouds that move
      In liquid air.

III.

Let them adore the Lord,
  And praise His holy name,
By whose almighty word
  They all from nothing came;
      And all shall last,
    From changes free;
    His firm decree
      Stands ever fast.

IV.

Let earth her tribute pay:
  Praise him ye dreadful whales,
And fish that through the sea
  Glide swift with glitt'ring scales;

Fire, hail, and snow,
And misty air,
And winds that where
He bids them blow.

The dedicating officer gives one rap and all are seated, and if there is to be an oration, this is the time to deliver it; or the Knights give the Taborian drill, and the ceremony closes.

SECOND DIAGRAM.

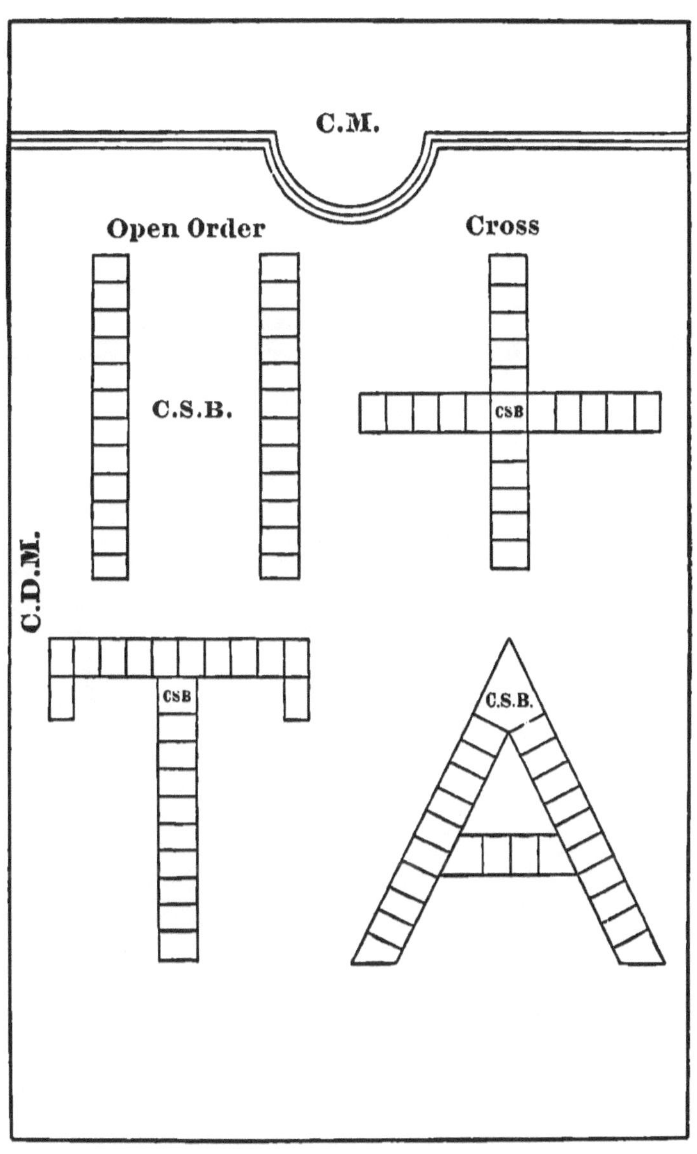

INSPECTION DIAGRAM.

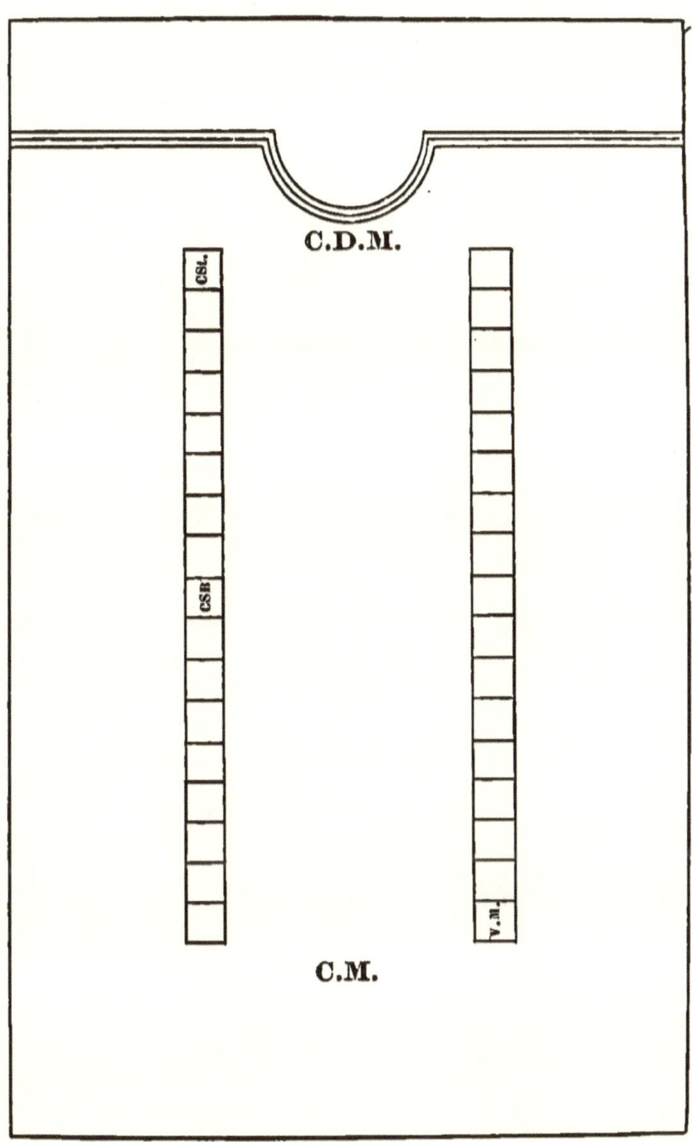

TACTICS AND DRILL

FOR THE USE OF THE

KNIGHTS OF TABOR.

DIAGRAM NO. 3.

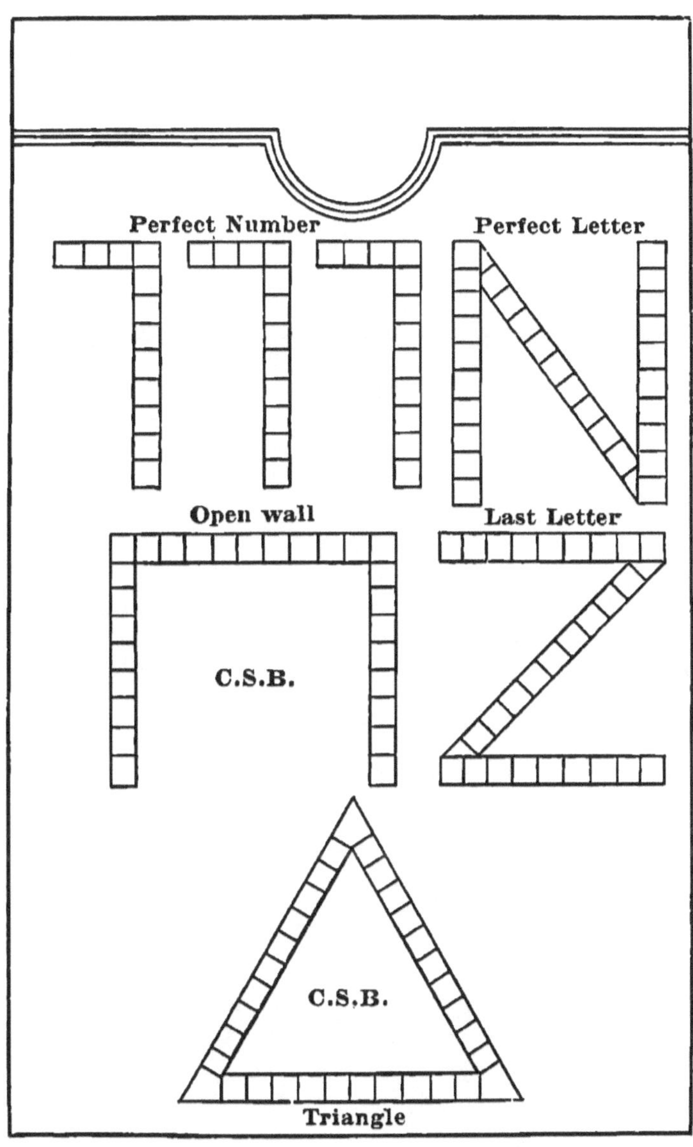

Perfect Number
Perfect Letter
Open wall
Last Letter
C.S.B.
C.S.B.
Triangle

TACTICS AND DRILL

FOR THE USE OF THE

KNIGHTS OF TABOR.

COMMAND.

1. Cautionary, which is: Attention, Sir Knights!

2. The preparatory, which indicates the movement.

3. The command of execution, which causes the movement.

POSITION.

1. Heels on the same line, as near as possible.
2. The feet turned out equally; stand easy.
3. The knees straight.
4. The body erect, inclining a little forward.
5. Shoulders square, and falling naturally.
6. The arms hanging, with elbows near the body.
7. The head erect and to the front.
8. The chin drawn in.
9. The eyes fixed straight to the front.
10. The tallest man to right of the line.
11. The smallest man to extreme left of the line.
12. Sir Knights will fall in, with swords in scabbard.

TO FORM LINES.

To form the lines, the C. D. M. will command:

1. Attention, Sir Knights! Fall In!

[The Knights will form in one rank, face to the right.]

2. Front Face!

[Raise the right foot slightly and turn on the left heel half-round, shoulders slightly touching.]

3. Right Dress!

[Each Knight will turn his head to the right and place himself on a line with the Sir Knight next to him on his right. The "left dress" is executed by the same movements reversed.]

4. Front!

[The head will resume the natural position.]

5. From the right, Count Twos!

[At this command the Sir Knights will count from right to left in a distinct voice, "One, Two; One, Two;" until through the ranks.]

6. Form divisions, Right Face!

[The Sir Knights will all face to the right; division No. 2 will place itself on the right of No. 1, thus forming the Sir Knights into files of two abreast, Nos. 1 constituting the first division and Nos. 2 the second.]

7. Officers in Ranks!

[At this command the V. M. will take his place to the right of the second division, the C. S. to the right of the first division, the C. S. B. in the centre.]

8. Form Lines and Receive the C. M.!

The V. M. will command:

9. Second Division, By file left, March!

[At this command the second division will march promptly to the left.]

10. By file left, March!

[Until they arrive opposite the first division, the V. M. will command. After placing his division exactly opposite the first division by right or left dress, he will resume his place to the right of his division. While this movement is being executed, the C. S. will command the first division.]

11. (1) Mark Time! (2) Frònt!

12. First Division, Front! Right Dress! Front!

[The Sir Knights will thus be formed in two parallel lines, facing inward. The C. D. M. advances to the C. M.'s station, salutes, and says: Sir Chief, the lines are now ready for inspection.]

The C. M. takes his place to the right between the two divisions, standing firm. The C. D. M. commands:

13. Attention, Sir Knights! Handle Swords! Draw Swords! Carry Swords! Salute the C. M.! Present Swords!

The C. M. passes down through the lines and takes his place on the extreme left, and commands:

14. Sir Knights, Carry Swords!
15. Sir Knights, Form Wall of Steel!
16. Sir Knights, Take Taborian Position!
17. Sir Knights, Carry Swords!

18. Sir Knights, Present Swords!
19. Sir Knights, Guard the Head!
20. Sir Knights, Guard the Body!
21. Sir Knights, Form a Wall of Steel!
22. Sir Knights, Carry Swords!
23. Sir Knights, Present Swords!
24. Sir Knights, Carry Comrade!
25. Sir Knights, Give the Taborian Rest!
26. Sir Knights, Salute!
27. Sir Knights, Return Swords!

The C. D. M. commands:

28. Sir Knights, Present Swords!

The C. M. passes up through the lines and takes his seat.

29. Sir Knights, Return Swords!

MARCHING DRILL.

The C. D. M. commands.

30. Second Division, Left Face!
31. First Division, Right Face!
32. Second Division, By file right, March! [They march until they reach the proper place at the right of the first division.]
33. Second Division, Halt!
34. Sir Knights, Mark Time!

[Always step off on your left foot.]

35. Sir Knights, By file right, March!

[At each turn that is made, repeat command, By file right.]

36. March down the centre of the hall.

37. First Division, File Right; Second Division, File Left, March!

This movement separates the divisions — and unites them — in their march and countermarch around the hall.

38. First Division, By file left, March!

39. Second Division, By file right, March!

[As they march around the hall and pass each other, they present swords.]

40. First Division, By file right, March!

[This movement places it by the side of the second division.]

41. Form Taborian Cross.

[This is formed by the odd numbers 15, 17, or 21. It will take some practice, and every man must know his place. When the command is given, ten Knights in the second division form across the hall, and eleven Knights of the first division march in, and thus form the Cross. *See diagram.*]

42. Form Taborian T.

[The same twenty-one Knights form the T — the second division horizontal, and the first division perpendicular. *See diagram.*]

43. Form Taborian A.

[Nine of the second division form the left line, and ten of the first form the right line, and one from each division form the centre. They march with arms folded. *See diagram.*]

44. Divisions, Form in Open Order!

[*See diagram.*]

45. Sir Knights, Form in Single File!

[The second division marches around and falls in the rear of the first division,—the first division marking time.]

46. Sir Knights, Halt! Front Face! Right Dress!

TO FORM THREE DIVISIONS.

47. Sir Knights, Count by Threes!

[At this command, the Knights will count from right to left: "One, Two, Three; One, Two, Three"—thus through the line.]

The C. D. M. will now command:

48. Sir Knights, Form Divisions; Right Face!

[The Sir Knights will face to the right, and No. 2 will take position to the right of No. 1, and No. 3 will take position to the right of No. 2. Mark time.]

49. Forward, March!

50. Open Order!

[At this command the Knights will take positions from three to seven feet apart, to the right and left.]

There are several fancy positions that can be taken by these divisions, but care must be had that each Knight knows his proper place. Do not attempt them in public until you can go through them perfectly in the hall.

51. Form the Perfect Number—777!

[The Three Sevens cannot be formed with less

than twenty-seven Knights. When the order is given, three Knights from each division, by one backward step, from the right or left, take position to the left. *See diagram.*]

52. Sir Knights, Resume your Places in Divisions!

53. Sir Knights, Form the Perfect Letter N!

[To form this letter properly, the divisions must be seven feet apart. The second division will rest their right upon the right of the first division, and their left upon the left of the third division. *See diagram.*]

54. Sir Knights, Resume Places and Close Up Ranks!

There are several other beautiful positions that can be taken by these divisions:

The Triangle — △.

The Open Wall — ⊓.

The Letter Z.

[*See diagram.*]

TO FORM FOUR DIVISIONS.

55. Attention, Sir Knights; Fall In!

[Always fall in with face to the right.]

The C. D. M. commands:

56. Front Face!

57. Right Dress!

58. From the Right, Count by Fours!

59. Form Divisions; Right Face!

[No. 2 will quickly take place to the right of No. 1, No. 3 to the right of No. 2, No. 4 to the right of No. 3.]

These divisions can be thrown into many fancy positions, and the C. D. M. can exercise his skill in maneuvering the Sir Knights. (1) Open Columns; (2) Two Divisions; (3) Three Divisions; (4) Four Divisions; (5) The Hollow Square; (6) The Double Square ˥L; (7) The letter "M," and various other fancies.

NOTICE.

To become perfect in the Tactics and Drill, we must practice regular, and all must attend if they would perform well. One balk will throw the entire divisions in confusion.

SWORD EXERCISE.

60. Draw Swords!

[First Motion.—At the word "draw," seize the scabbard with the left hand and grasp the sword with the right hand, and draw it out two inches.

Second Motion.—At the word "swords," draw the sword from the scabbard and extend the right hand to the front, and drop the sword in the hollow of the elbow.

Third Motion.—Bring the right hand to the thigh, the elbow a little bent, holding the sword between the thumb and two fingers, the blade perpendicular, being position of "Carry Swords."]

61. Present Swords!

[Raise the sword perpendicularly, the flat of the blade opposite the right eye, the guard at the height of the shoulder, and the elbow supported on the body.]

62. Carry Swords!

[Extend the hand to the front and replace the sword, as in the second and third motions of "Draw Swords."]

63. Taborian Position!

[First Motion. — Same as "Present Swords!

Second Motion. — Drop the point of the sword by extending the arm, so that the right hand will rest on the right side of the thigh, the point of the sword resting on the floor or ground, about eighteen inches from the right foot; the Knight to your right takes position, his left foot touching the sword.]

64. Guard the Head!

[First Motion. — Same as "Present Swords."

Second Motion. — Hold the sword in a horizontal position above the head, about six inches in front of the forehead.]

65. Guard the Body!

[First Motion. — Same as "Present Swords," except in this case the blade is outward.

Second Motion. — Cut downward, and bring the sword to carry.]

66. Form a Wall of Steel!

[First Motion. — Same as "Present Swords."

Second Motion. — Bring your sword down horizontal, the right hand resting on the centre of the breast, the point of your sword resting on the breast of the Knight to your left.]

67. Carry Comrade!

[First Motion. — Present swords.

Second Motion. — Lay your sword across your shoulders and grasp the point with your left hand.]

68. Taborian Rest!

[First Motion. — Present swords.

Second Motion. — Rest the sword in the hollow of the elbow joint, and grasp the blade near the guard with the left hand.]

69. Salute!

[First Motion. — Present swords.]

[Second Motion. — Drop the point of the sword by extending the arm, so that the right hand may be brought to the side of the right thigh, the nails up, the elbow well back from the body.]

70. Return Swords!

[First Motion. — Bring the sword to the position of "Present," and seize the scabbard with the left hand near its mouth.

Second Motion. — Drop the point; turn the head to the left, and return the sword; bring your head to front, and drop the hands to their natural position by the side.]

71. Sir Knights, Disperse; Return to Quarters!

JAVELIN DRILL.

The javelins are made about seven feet in length, steel-pointed, and one inch in diameter. When the javelins are used, the swords are not worn.

The ranks are formed in the same manner as in the Inspection diagram.

INSPECTION.

The Chief Drill-Master addresses the Chief Mentor:

Sir Chief, the Knights are ready for inspection.

The Chief steps to the right front. The C. D. M. commands:

1. Attention, Sir Knights! Form Arch!

[First Motion. — Present javelins, holding them about one foot from the heel of the javelin.

Second Motion. — Carry the right foot about eighteen inches to the front; extend the javelin arm, and cross the head of the javelin, about three inches from the point, with that of the Sir Knight opposite.]

The C. M. passes down through the ranks slowly. On arriving at the extreme left, he turns and faces to the right. The C. M. commands:

2. Sir Knights, Ground Javelins!

[First Motion. — Present javelins, and bring the feet together.

Second Motion. — Let the javelin slide down the right side until the heels rest on the ground (or floor), holding it between the thumb and two fingers; arm extended down, javelin resting against the right shoulder.]

3. Sir Knights, Repel Javelins!

[First Motion. — Grasp the javelin about the centre, and present.

Second Motion. — Drop the javelin hand to the

right hip, and let it firmly rest there, the point of the javelin to the front, and the heel to the rear,—the point about one foot higher than the heel. Advance the left foot about eighteen inches.]

4. Carry Javelins!

[First Motion.—Present javelins, grasping the javelin about one foot above the heel.

Second Motion.—Drop the hand behind, so that it will rest on the right small of the back, nails out; arm over the javelin point, above the head; javelin near the right side of the face.]

5. Take Position, Right and Left!

[First Motion.—Grasp the javelin about the centre, and present.

Second Motion.—Bring the hand to the breast, so that the javelin will extend horizontally across the breast. The first division will side-step to the right, and the second division will side-step to the left, until the point and heel just touch the Knights on either side.]

6. Poise Javelins!

[First Motion.—Present, grasping the centre of the javelin.

Second Motion.—Rest the javelin in the hollow between the thumb and forefinger; raise the hand until it is on a level with the right eye, and point front.]

7. Ascend Mount Tabor!

[First Motion.—Bring the javel into a present with the right hand about eighteen inches from the heel.

Second Motion.—Grasp the javelin with the left

hand, near the centre, and let the right hand rest on the hip; elevate the point about one foot. Keep time, or imitate walking.]

8. Division, Rest!

[First Motion. — Bring the javelin to a present.

Second Motion. — Rest the heel, and lean the point on the right shoulder, and grasp the javelin with both hands.]

9. Present Javelins!

10. Right Face!

11. Mount Javelins!

[Throw the javelin across the shoulders, and grasp it with both hands.]

12. Present Javelins!

13. Front Face!

14. Right About Face!

15. Repel Javelins!

16. Present Javelins!

17. Left About Face!

18. Form Arch!

The C. M. passes up through the ranks to his station, and the C. D. M. takes command, and may exercise in marching or division drill, or disperse.

FORMS, DECISIONS, AND RULES.

TEMPLE

BY-LAWS AND REGULATIONS.

ARTICLE I.

SECTION 1. This Temple shall be known by the name of ——— Temple, No. —.

ARTICLE II.

TIME TO ASSEMBLE.

SECTION 1. The hour to assemble shall be —— o'clock, P. M., in the winter months, and —— o'clock, P. M., in the spring and autumn, and —— o'clock, P. M., in the summer.

ARTICLE III.

FEES AND DUES.

SECTION 1. The fees for the degrees shall be as follows: . . . . $—; for the Widows and Orphans' Fund, $—. The fee must come with the petition, or it cannot be acted on.

SEC. 2. Monthly dues per month shall be ——, in advance. When members permit their dues to remain unpaid for three consecutive months, the C. S. shall announce the name of the member at any regular meeting, stating that the member is three months in arrears. If said member fails to pay within thirty days after the announcement, he forfeits his rights to all the benefits of the Temple until all dues and assessments are paid.

Sec. 3. A member who is suspended for a definite or an indefinite time forfeits his right to all the benefits of the Temple until he is restored.

Sec. 4. A member who is expelled is dead to every right and privilege, and forfeits his right to all the benefits of the Temple until he is restored by action of the Temple, at a special meeting, and a notice of the restoration given to the C. G. S.

ARTICLE IV.

BENEFITS.

Section 1. Each member in good standing shall be entitled to and receive $— per week during the time he is under the care of a physician.

Sec. 2. It is provided, however, that before a member can receive these benefits, he must have been a member in good standing for at least ——— months.

Sec. 3. Read Article VI. of the Constitution for further information.

ARTICLE V.

FINES.

Section 1. It is not the intention of the founders of the Temple, in giving a code of laws, to compel Sir Knights to do their duty; that is made plain by their obligation, constitutions, regulations, and rules. A Sir Knight who will not do his plain duty without being compelled, is not fit to remain a member of the Temple; therefore, these fines are not assessed to make Sir Knights better, but for neglect or forgetfulness of duty:

1. For a failure to meet a regular assembly, and not having a lawful excuse.

2. For not being present at the hour of opening, not having a lawful excuse.

3. For not attending at the bedside of a sick or disabled Sir Knight, when ordered by the C. M., not having a lawful excuse.

4. For not attending the funeral of a Sir Knight, not having a lawful excuse.

5. For not coming to order when requested by the C. M.

6. All fines must be paid within three months after they are assessed; for neglecting to pay, unless otherwise ordered by the Temple, at a regular meeting, the member shall be suspended until his fine is paid.

ARTICLE VI.

THE MEETINGS.

Section 1. The regular meetings of the Temple shall be on the ——— of each month. There shall be twelve regular meetings each year. The assembly must be opened in regular form, and closed the same night.

A LAWFUL EXCUSE.

Sec. 2. Absence from the city, sickness in the family, or in person.

Read the Constitution carefully.

TABERNACLE

BY-LAWS AND REGULATIONS.

ARTICLE I.

NAME.

SECTION 1. This Tabernacle shall be known by the name of ——, No. —.

ARTICLE II.

MEETINGS.

SECTION 1. The regular meetings shall be held on the —— —— of each month, at — o'clock —.

SEC. 2. There shall be twelve regular meetings held during the year, and called meetings when ordered by the C..P.

ARTICLE III.

FEES AND DUES.

SECTION 1. The fees for the degrees shall be as follows: . . . . $—.
No petition shall be acted on unless the fee is paid.

SEC. 2. Every member shall pay —— cents monthly, in advance. [For further information on this subject, see Constitution, Article VIII.]

ARTICLE IV.

BENEFITS.

SECTION 1. Each member in good standing shall be entitled to and receive $—— per week, during the time she is under the care of a physician; provided, however, that before a member can receive these benefits she must have been a member in good standing at least —— months. [For further information on this subject, read Article XVI. of the Constitution.]

SEC. 2. Refers to Article VII. of the Constitution.

ARTICLE V.

FINES.

Every member is equally interested in the success and good name of the Tabernacle. A united effort is required on the part of the members to make the Order a success.

SECTION 1. Fulfil every duty and obligation that is required of you, earnestly and constantly.

SEC. 2. A member failing to be present at a regular meeting, and not having a lawful excuse, shall be fined ——.

SEC. 3. For not being present at the hour of opening, not having a lawful excuse, the member shall be fined ——.

SEC. 4. For not attending at the bedside of a sick

or disabled Daughter, when ordered by the C. P., not having a lawful excuse, the member shall be fined ——.

Sec. 5. For not attending the funeral of a Daughter, not having a lawful excuse, the member shall be fined ——.

Sec. 6. For not coming to order when requested by the C. P., the fine shall be ——.

Sec. 7. All fines must be paid within three months after they are assessed. For neglecting to pay, unless otherwise ordered by the Tabernacle at a regular meeting, the member shall be suspended until the fines are paid.

Sec. 8. Sickness in the family or absence from the city are lawful excuses.

Read the Constitution carefully.

FORM OF KEEPING THE JOURNAL OF BUSINESS.

——, A. D. 18—.

—— Temple, No.—, of the Knights of Tabor, assembled —— the —— A. O. T. —— at — o'clock, P. M., and opened in the —— degree. Officers all on duty, except (naming the office). The C. M. appointed Sir Knights —— to attend to their duties *pro tem*.

If it is a stated meeting, proceed with the rules.

1. The proceedings of the last regular and intervening meetings are read, corrected, and adopted.

2. The Board of Attendants make a report, as follows: . . . . On motion, it was received and adopted.

3. The Board of Judges make a report, as follows: . . . . On motion, it was referred back (or adopted).

4. The petition of Mr. ——— was read, and, on motion, it was received.

5. The petition of Mr. ——— was balloted on, and he was elected (or rejected).

The roll was called, and dues collected as follows:

Monthly dues..............................	$00 00
Taxes......................................	00 00
Fines......................................	00 00
Petition-money...........................	00 00
Total received..........................	$000 00
Brought forward........................	$000 00
Total in treasury.......................	$000 00

Amount paid out, —

For (name what it is paid out for)........	$00 00
For " " " "	00 00
For " " " "	00 00
For " " " "	00 00
Total paid out..........................	$000 00
Balance in treasury....................	$000 00

6. If there was any unfinished business left over from the last or intervening meetings, attend to it, and let the minutes show what it was, and what was done.

7. The minutes must show all the new business that was done.

8. The reports of special committees.

9. The correspondence is read and disposed of.

10. Special committees appointed.

11. The variety of business that must come up in the Temple or Tabernacle.

[I give this as an outline of how to keep the minutes of both Temple and Tabernacle.]

NOTICE.

With but slight alteration, this form will do for the Tabernacle.

FORM OF A PETITION FOR A CHARTER.

To the Chief Grand Mentor of the N. G. T.:

We, the undersigned, Knights of Tabor, holding withdrawal certificates from Temples legally chartered, would most respectfully state that we believe it would benefit our Order to open a Temple in . . . . county of . . . . State of . . . . We, your petitioners, respectfully ask that a charter be granted. We herewith nominate the following officers for your approval

1 . . . . C. M.	7 . . . . C. D. M.
2 . . . . V. M.	8 . . . . C. S. B.
3 . . . . C. S.	9 . . . . C. G.
4 . . . . A. S.	10 . . . . C. G.
5 . . . . C. T.	11 . . . . C. G.
6 . . . . C. O.	12 . . . . C. St.

Charter fee inclosed.................... $00 00

For books, blanks, etc................... 00 00

Total............................ $000 00

Recommended by . . . . D. G. M.

Dated this . . day of . . . . A. D. 18 . . A. O. T. . . . .

FORM OF A PETITION FOR A WARRANT.

To the Chief Grand Mentor of the N. G. T.:

We, the undersigned Daughters of the Tabernacle, having withdrawal certificates from warranted Tabernacles, and believing it will be for the interest of our Order to open a Tabernacle in . . . . county of . . . . State of . . . . we therefore ask that a warrant be granted. We have nominated the following officers for your approval:

1	C. P.	7	I. S.
2	V. P.	8	O. S.
3	C. R.	9	Tribune.
4	V. R.	10	Tribune.
5	C. T.	11	Tribune.
6	C.Pr.		

Inclosed warrant fee.................... $00 00
For books, blanks, etc.................... 00 00

Total........................... $00 00

Recommended by . . . . D. G. M.

Dated . . . . . A.D. . . . A. O. T. . . . . . .

DECISIONS.

THE POWERS AND PREROGATIVES OF THE CHIEF GRAND MENTOR.

1. He can preside at all meetings of the Grand Temple and Tabernacle.

2. He can assemble the Grand Temple and Tabernacle in special session whenever he determines it necessary.

3. He can suspend the laws, regulations, and rules of the Grand Temple and Tabernacle in all cases requiring temporary suspension.

4. He can confer the Temple and Tabernacle degrees, or deputize the authority by commission.

5. He can organize Temples and Tabernacles, either in person or by deputy.

6. He can constitute new Temples and Tabernacles by charter or warrant.

7. He can visit and preside in any Temple or Tabernacle.

8. He can suspend the work and business of a Temple or Tabernacle for a time, or until the next annual session of the Grand Temple.

9. He can suspend a Chief Mentor or a Chief Preceptress until the annual session of the Grand Temple, and fill their places by appointment.

10. He can preside as chairman of any committee that he honors by his presence.

11. He can decide all points of law, rules, and questions of order. His decisions hold good until they are reversed by his successor.

12. He can appoint officers *pro tem.*, in case of absence or neglect of the officers elected to attend to the official duties, or for disqualification.

13. He cannot alter the time of holding the National Grand Session, but he can — with the concurrence of a majority of the Temples and Tabernacles — change the place fixed upon for the Grand Session.

14. He can appoint as many District Deputies as, in his judgment, are required, and fix the limits of their districts.

15. He cannot remove an elected Grand Officer from official duty, except upon charges so grave that expulsion will be the result of a trial.

16. He can grant a charter to a Temple, or a warrant to a Tabernacle, upon proof that their charter or warrant has been lost or destroyed.

17. He cannot be disciplined for his official acts, after he has passed out of office.

NATIONAL GRAND TEMPLE.

The power and authority of the Grand Temple and Tabernacle are defined in Articles IV. and XII. of the Grand Temple Constitution.

SUBORDINATE TEMPLES.

It requires careful study of the Constitution to thoroughly understand how to administer the laws, rules, and regulations.

LADIES' TABERNACLE.

A strict compliance and obedience to the requirements of the Constitution will keep the Tabernacle in a healthy condition.

PRESIDING OFFICER.

In selecting a presiding officer for either Temple or Tabernacle, the members are responsible if they make a poor or a bad choice. The qualifications for a presiding officer are honesty, energy, intelligence, culture, and executive ability.

RULES OF ORDER.

---

1. The presiding officer, at the proper hour, takes his seat, and gives one rap; the officers and members clothe in regalia, and take their respective seats. The Temple is then opened in order.

2. The regular business of the Temple shall be done without a motion, as prescribed in the Rules of Business.

3. During the reading of the minutes, communications, or other papers, silence shall be observed. After they are read, the minutes, if they are correct, stand approved; if there is a question of their correctness, the member who questions their correctness shall state what is not correct, and move that the correction be made.

4. Members and visitors must come to the hall cleanly dressed, wearing the working regalia, and white gloves.

5. A member, when addressing the Temple, shall stand and address the C. M. as Sir Chief.

6. During the time that the Temple is open and

doing business, no refreshments, smoking, or chewing tobacco will be permitted.

7. When a C. G. M. or a P. C. G. M. visits the Temple, he must be received with the standing grand honors.

8. When a Grand Officer visits the Temple, he must be received standing.

9. All officers in open Temple shall be addressed by the title of their office, all members as Sir Knight; these titles to be used only in open Temple, or when on duty or parade.

10. When it is necessary to get the sense of the Temple on any question or resolution, it must be done by motion and second, stated by the presiding officer, and decided by the voting sign.

11. When an office is made vacant by death, resignation, or for any other cause, the C. M. shall appoint a member to fulfil the duties until the regular election.

12. The C. M. shall control the business of the Temple, and determine the time to close, without a motion.

13. The regular business of the Temple shall be done by the Rules of Business.

14. The C. M. shall be responsible to the Grand Temple for the manner in which he administers the laws of the Temple. He shall decide all doubtful

questions of Constitution, regulations, and order. His decision shall be final, until reversed by the C. G. M. or the Grand Temple.

15. No member shall speak more than once on the same subject, until all who wish to speak have spoken; nor more than twice, without permission from the C. M. No member shall speak longer than ten minutes, without permission from the C. M.

16. A member speaking shall stand in front of the Temple and address the chief officer, confine himself to the question, and avoid personalities and irrelevant language.

17. A member shall not be interrupted while speaking, except to explain.

18. A motion shall not be in order until it is seconded, and stated by the presiding officer. A motion must be made in writing, when requested by the C. S.

19. A motion to lie on the table shall be decided without debate.

20. A motion to postpone carries the question over to the next meeting.

21. When a question is laid on the table, it cannot be taken up until the next meeting, and then only by a two-thirds vote.

22. A motion to reconsider can be acted upon

only at the same session; it must be made by a member who voted in the majority.

23. The first named on all special committees shall be the chairman.

24. In all business meetings they shall proceed by the Order of Business.

25. A member wishing to retire from the meeting for the evening, must come before the Temple, and make the request to the C. M. He announces the request, and if a majority vote to grant, it is done.

26. Members wishing to retire for a few minutes, rise from their seats and stand, with the saluting sign; the C. M. observes them, and returns the sign, — that is permission granted.

27. A member crossing the hall during the time the Temple is opened must give the saluting sign.

28. The strictest order and decorum must be kept during the hour of the session.

29. Should an officer be absent from a meeting, the C. M. shall fill the seat *pro tem.*

30. A motion for indefinite postponement, if decided in the affirmative, quashes the proposition entirely, and is not debatable.

31. A motion, when regularly made and seconded, and proposed from the chair, cannot be withdrawn without the consent of the assembly.

INDEX.

ENGRAVINGS.

www.ingramcontent.com/pod-product-compliance
Lightning Source LLC
Chambersburg PA
CBHW030803020726
47499CB00006B/1746

* 9 7 8 3 3 3 7 2 8 6 7 7 4 *